A Dove's Cry

A Dove's Cry

K. McCoy

Published by K. McCoy, 2021.

A DOVE'S CRY

First edition. December 25, 2021.

ISBN: 979-8218017262

Written by K. McCoy.

Table of Contents

"Rejoice in hope, be patient in tribulation, be constant in prayer."

A DOVE'S CRY

Written by K. McCoy

Chapter One
Party Crashers

Jerome

Stepping out of his car and looking around, Jerome made sure all the doors were locked before heading inside the gentlemen's club. Seeing the name *Bottoms Up* in vivid lights, Jerome knew he was in the right place. It was almost eleven, and all he wanted to do was go home and go to bed, but if this is where his friend wanted to celebrate his bachelor party, who was he to judge?

Walking through the double black doors, Jerome checked his pockets for his ID and cash to pay the entrance fee. He tried his best to look the women sashaying around him in the eye, but with the fog and flashing lights, he found it hard to focus. The guard that patted him down for any contraband before letting him through the next set of doors laughed. "Don't have too much fun in there, virgin blood."

He could see the shock on all his friends' faces as he walked up to them at their VIP table. No one said anything at first until the man of the hour walked over and gave Jerome a side hug.

"Jerome! Fancy seeing you here," Wyatt shouted over the music.

"No doubt! I thought the least I could do was come through."

Jerome saw a woman take the stage, and he blinked several times at the speed and agility she displayed as she climbed up and spun around on the silver pole. When he turned back to face his friend again, all the guys at the table were leaning against one another, laughing hysterically.

"Tonight is going to be a good night, fellas! We got the golden preacher boy to join us at BU. Let's drink!" Patrick, Wyatt's best man, held up his drink as the others brought their glasses together for the toast.

Guess I better order something, Jerome thought to himself.

Cutting through the guys and walking toward the nearest bar, he waited until the bartender noticed him before leaning in to be heard over the music.

"What can I get for you, suga?" the short woman asked.

He scanned the bar station. "I'll just have a grape soda pop."

The woman looked him over slowly before she went to get his drink. "It's five dollars, baby."

Jerome handed her a ten-dollar bill. "Keep the change."

That earned him a wicked grin from the bartender. "I was gonna anyway!"

Turning around and sipping from his bottled drink, Jerome counted four women now in their section. As he parted his way through the VIP crowd, the girls acknowledged him with a few winks and alluring smiles. One of them, a chick with golden brown skin and braids that went to her bottom, swayed over to him and sat close enough to Jerome that one of her thighs overlapped onto one of his knees.

"You new to the Bottom?" she asked sweetly.

Jerome answered honestly, "Yeah. How did you know?"

She looked at the others from his crew and then back at him. "I ain't seen you before, and those goons are here every payday."

He nodded and extended his hand to the woman. "My name's Jerome. It's nice to meet you."

The woman fluttered her eyelashes at him, making Jerome expose all his teeth. "Nice to meet you, Jerome. I'm Velvet." She took his hand in hers and shook it gingerly. "If you want a special dance later, don't see the rest. Come straight to the best, ya hear?" she told him.

"O-okay then. I will remember that, Velvet."

Jerome had no intentions of asking or receiving a dance later, but he didn't want to be rude. To thank her for her time, Jerome then reached into his pocket and pulled out a five-dollar bill and handed it to her. She held the bill up to the light to inspect it as she stood up to leave. Brushing her braids across Jerome's knees, Velvet turned to face him again and blew him a kiss. The other girls in their VIP section were watching the exchange between them, and Jerome wasn't sure if that was a good or bad thing. As she strolled away, Velvet shouted over to the guys in his section, "Finally! A fucking real man showed up to this bitch!"

All the guys looked at Jerome as Mitch, his friend from high school, yelled at him while smoking a cigarette, "Yo man! You suppose to give them money *after* the lap dance, not before!"

The others laughed as Jerome sipped his drink.

Almost an hour had passed, and everyone was still in good spirits. Jerome had finished his drink a while ago but didn't want to get up again, as he noticed that when men were up and about, the women not on stage latched on to them, enticing them into buying a dance. To make use of that time, Jerome instead talked to the fellas about the upcoming church jamboree.

Some of the guys must have gotten sick of him bringing it up, as they eventually agreed to volunteer to help set up and man a few stations during the event. Jerome typed their phone numbers into his phone and started to enjoy the atmosphere like everyone else. He nodded in time to the music playing in the club and opened the text app to his phone.

Hey, I get it - no one wants to look lame not getting it.
But think about it, is it really worth it?
When you finally find your wife and she asks, "What's your body count?"

He had found a decent flow when Jerome felt a soft tap on his shoulder.

"Thought you could use another drink." The bartender from earlier had another bottled soda in her hand, and she reached over the small rail to hand it to Jerome.

"Thanks. You ain't have to do that," he told her earnestly as he took the drink from her.

While he was digging in his pockets for money to pay her, she asked him, "What ya doing with your phone out? You know the bouncers here will kick your ass if you take pics of the girls," she warned him.

Jerome shook his head. "Nah sister, nothing like that. I just got an idea for a verse and wanted to get it down before it was gone, I swear."

She tilted her head before tapping on the screen of his phone. "Can I see what you came up with?"

Jerome's eyes widened. "You ain't gonna clown me if it's whack, are you?"

The bartender chuckled, "We'll just have to wait and see, uh?"

Looking around to make sure his crew was busy with the dancers, Jerome entered his PIN code and turned his phone toward her to show what he had jotted down a moment ago. To keep himself busy from possibly being laughed at, Jerome started to lightly tap his heel against the back of the couch that he was sitting on and waited for her to say something.

"I wasn't expecting that," she told him.

Jerome looked her in the eye and asked hopefully, "Is that a good thing or a bad thing?"

The bartender held his stare. "Just what kind of rapper you trying to be in these streets?"

"I want to be a Christian rapper. You know, inspire and help someone find their light," Jerome answered nervously. He waited for her to laugh, but when she slowly nodded and walked away, Jerome called out to her, "Wait! I didn't pay for my drink."

The bartender turned around and smiled. "You gave me something tonight worth more than money in this joint. We even."

He was left to just stare as she went back behind the bar to make drinks for a few of the girls that were in between dances. *I guess she liked it?*

TASHA

Tasha was working at the The Fast Fix food truck while in between jobs, thanks to one of her oldest friends, Alexa. She really didn't mind the work. For one, it was mostly quiet, and she got to work alone. Also, her homegirl always sent that direct deposit on time.

It's a lot better than working retail, she thought dryly.

The main reason she liked this new gig was that she hardly ran into anyone that she had gone to school with. It wasn't like Tasha was voted 'Most Likely to Succeed' or anything, but after high school she was supposed to have been up and gone from this backwards town. She did everything she could to make that happen, but it still wasn't enough. When Tasha got accepted to her dream college during her senior year, she was on cloud nine for days. Then, with one visit from financial aid weeks later, all her hopes and dreams came crashing down. Tasha wandered around town feeling like a complete failure for a year before finally getting herself together.

Instead of leaving town, Tasha found herself struggling to pay tuition at her local community college. With two part-time jobs and a work study on campus, she couldn't keep money in her account for nothing! But she was making it work, even if it meant she only slept on the weekends.

Then, in the middle of her senior year at Grover Community College, she was blindsided by the news of her family being in financial trouble and about to lose the home that Tasha grew up in. Her sisters apparently had been out of work for months and didn't tell her. But they came to her a month before the bank was due to foreclose on their childhood home.

Tasha then spent her last night in her tiny studio apartment, eating ice cream and quietly crying until she fell asleep. Selling what she could from her apartment, she ended her lease and went to withdraw from GCC. She moved back home and worked double shifts when she could at whatever job would hire her so she could make the new payments with the bank. Two weeks after Tasha moved back home, her older sister, Tina, finally got a job, and that helped them get caught up. All of this happened years ago, but whenever someone she went to school with saw Tasha, her still being in town was the first and only thing they would want to talk about. And it still made her angry as hell.

To deal with her pain, Tasha started taking photos. Nothing fancy really, just another way for her to express herself. Until one day at a local park, she took a photo of a woman about the same age as her mama. The woman, Joanna, asked to see the photo, and when Tasha showed it to her, Joanna asked her how soon could she could have it printed and framed. Tasha had no idea what she meant at first, but she found out real quick that same day and made her first sale.

It was enough to pay the mortgage that month! Tasha remembered fondly.

Three months later, she had created a website, quit one of her temp jobs, and slowly started to take on clients. She had loved studying English in school, but learning about photography felt more like her true calling.

Plus, I get to choose who I work with and my prices per session!

Tasha grinned as she scrolled through her phone, looking for new photography equipment to add to her gear bag. Most of the items that Tasha drooled over these days she couldn't afford to pay for in full, so she added them to her wish list. Once she did that, Tasha made a mental note to check and see if the local photoshop in the mall near her place had any of the things she wanted that could be put on a leasing plan. Hearing the closing song from inside the club, Tasha sat up to turn the fryer back on.

Time to feed the horny herd, Tasha thought to herself as she watched the dudes stumble outside.

Only a few folks were interested in something greasy tonight, so she quickly worked to serve them their food and watched as the last group of customers hopped into their cars to leave. With the club officially closed, the girls exited from the back with the main bouncers. Tasha still looked at them in awe as she saw their transformations from 'club girl' to normal. She took in their much more comfortable attire of track suits, flat shoes, and hoodies before wondering again just how they managed to make that kind of change each night.

Some guys from a bachelor party group were lingering around as the girls were waiting to be picked up by their loved ones. Two of the guys separated from their pack and started coming on hard to the girls, and Tasha's stank face settled in before she could stop herself. Thinking quickly, she remembered the wings that Alexa said she could take home. She got the girls' attention by playing one of their favorite hype songs and waving the freshly fried goods from her window.

"Thought y'all might wanna try the new mango madness batch before your rides get here," she called out through her order window. Seeing the newest girl in the group inhale and then frown, Tasha added, "No worries, Rookie. I got a vegan batch with your name on it."

Satisfied with the distance between the girls and the guys, Tasha started to clean up for the night. But as she turned around to make sure the fryer was turned off, she heard one girl scream. Quickly making her way back to the service window, Tasha saw the same two guys from before grabbing Rookie's wrists as the other girls tried calling the after-hours bouncer for help. Flipping on the security lights on top of the truck and grabbing her portable siren, Tasha pressed the red button and waited for all the commotion to die down before she spoke. "I don't know who raised y'all, but manhandling women ain't a good look. Find somewhere else to be 'fore I throw on my Karen voice and have the city dogs out here!"

A third guy made his way next to the two dudes still near the newer girl. Tasha briefly wondered just how he fit into their little entourage, as he didn't seem to be bothered with wearing his worth out loud as the others did. He met her eye and spoke calmly, "Sister, that won't be necessary. We were just leaving, right fellas?"

The other two nodded quickly.

He seemed to be a standup guy, but if life had taught Tasha anything at twenty-six, it was that it only took one time for a dude to fuck around and ruin a chick's world if you let him. Her face hardened as she upped the watts on the security lights while directing them at the three men.

"You say y'all leaving but I don't see y'all walking away."

Rookie rushed toward the truck with the remaining girls and watched the two guys finally get into their limo.

"We was just asking what her prices were!" The music then blared as their limo took off into the night.

"Again, I'm sorry about my friends. Take care, sister," Jerome said before he got into his car and left.

With all the commotion over, the girls remained near The Fast Fix truck and started their nightly ritual of telling their worst-customer-of-the-night stories. One by one, each girl disappeared as someone showed up in a different vehicle to take them home. Rookie's ride was the last to get there. Before she hopped into her sister's jeep, she leaned over into the window of the service truck.

"Hey! Tash!" she shouted into the truck, getting Tasha to turn around.

"Yeah?"

"Thank you. Those guys were bugging me all night. Almost left early 'cause of them, but tuition just went up again this semester, so I had to stick it out."

"I hear that! Don't let no dude get in the way of your education. Or ya money!" Tasha reminded Rookie.

"You right, sis. Anyway, thanks again. Goodnight!"

"Night!"

JEROME

Getting ready for work took more out of him than usual. *How do they always stay out so late? Never again, Lord!* He thought to himself as he finished his breakfast.

A few guys did give him their contact information for the church jamboree

event, so he was happy about that. And things weren't all that bad, at least not until closing time when two of the guys got out of line with one of the girls.

Jerome thought Jesus himself was coming to round them all up for their heathen behavior when those truck lights hit his face. Laughing at the memory, he shook his head.

I gotta get out more, if a few flashing lights was all it took to spook me.

If he was honest with himself, Jerome would admit that it was more than the flashing lights. He'd grown up with those guys and gone to the same schools, but he felt like a stranger whenever he spent time with them away from the church. Being the son of a pastor was hard, especially since the only person that he ever felt he could talk to about anything left town over ten years ago. When he would go out to any event away from Christ's Corner, Jerome noticed early on how folks would change the conversation or avoid looking his way. It became painfully obvious his freshman year of college, when he thought about pledging to the fraternity on campus. He remembered standing alone at his first mixer, as some of the same guys who attended his church walked by with their girlfriends and friends. He could still hear their laughter as they strolled past him that night. That was seven years ago, and it still made his chest tighten to even think about it.

For the last few years, he enjoyed having his own place, but lately found a new kind of loneliness setting in. At least when he lived with his folks, there was his mama to talk to at the end of the day. Since college, all Senior ever did was tell him that his dreams of being a rapper were foolish and a waste of time.

But Jerome knew what he wanted, and this year was the year that he would make it happen.

Tasha

She had only agreed to this meeting because her boss promised it would be worth her while. So far, Tasha was not on board with the meeting's true agenda. Her close friends, Alexa and Rachel, stared at Tasha while holding hands as she looked over the rental contract in front of her.

"No. No way," she said as she finally pushed the documents away.

Rachel sighed as Alexa tried to soften the situation. "You'd be in a nicer part of town. Weren't you just saying how you wanted to move out of your family's house?"

"I wouldn't call that a house..." Rachel mumbled.

Alexa elbowed Rachel, but Tasha just laughed. "You're right, it's not really much of a house. But it's what I can afford."

Standing up, Tasha smiled at her friends and handed back their rental agreement. "I would love to come on as a roommate with y'all, but there's no way I can pay that amount each month. Sorry."

Before she could walk away, Rachel grabbed her wrist. "Please consider it Tash. We've been looking for another roommate for weeks, and Alexa's picky ass has rejected everyone I've considered except you."

Alexa and Rachel had been together for years now, ever since Alexa came back home after studying law in college. Tasha had never seen her girl so happy as she was with Rachel by her side. She should have known that they would be looking for a new roommate after hearing that Leela, Rachel's soror, decided to take a new job on the west coast. And as far back as their sophomore year of high school, Tasha and Alexa have been friends. So she knew exactly what Rachel was going through. Tasha thought back to their junior year, remembering when Alexa stopped eating at the school cafeteria after seeing one of the lunch ladies refilling the roll basket without a sneeze guard mask covering her nose. She almost laughed out loud from thinking back to those days, but she managed to keep a straight face. Seeing the silent eye battle between the two lovers, Tasha smiled again once the two looked back at her.

"I'm flattered, for real. But I just started leasing new gear, and without a steady job right now it wouldn't be smart for me to move in with y'all now."

"What if we could help you find more work?"

Tasha lowered her head. *Why won't they just let me grovel away already!*

"Really, the extra hours at the food truck have been hella helpful, but I don't want to inconvenience you anymore."

Alexa's eyes widened as she let go of Rachel's hand and grabbed her scheduler.

Oh Lawd! I know that look! She's already got something in mind. Dang overachiever!

"Wait! Here... got it! You can tutor at the church near our complex!"

Rachel nodded gleefully and kissed Alexa on the cheek. "That's right! I forgot about that offer."

"The pastor reached out to our office to help them find someone qualified for a tutoring position that they were opening up soon. You'd be great for this!"

Tasha looked down at the two hopeful faces and sighed. "Give me the contract again."

Hearing their squeals, Tasha shushed them as she reviewed the deposit and monthly rent amounts one last time. "I will call them, and if we can work something out, I'll let y'all know by the end of the week, cool?"

"Yea!" they said in unison.

"Okay then... potential roomies."

The two laughed as Tasha got up and left the restaurant.

SEEING THE MAIN DOOR to her childhood home open in the middle of the day always filled Tasha with dread.

Nothing good ever came from the sight.

Her dark feelings were getting stronger and stronger as she smelled a group of older women, scantily clad in club wear, who were staring at her as she walked through the front door.

It's mid-afternoon! Why are they coming down from their highs here?!

"Oh...you must be one of Kitty's girls!" one of them said as they pointed at her.

"Yes ma'am."

They laughed, but to Tasha the sound felt like razor blades churning and cutting up the inside of her stomach.

"So polite and PROPER! How'd Kitty get such a baby girl in her life?"

The one closest to Tasha squinted before reaching out and grabbing at her stomach. "Baby girl?! She look like she 'bout to have a baby herself in a few months!"

Their laughs continued as Tasha's eyes landed on her room door. Barely above a whisper, she spoke again. "Where is my mama?"

"Oh, you know, she went with her new friend . . . what was his name?" one woman answered casually. Tasha's blood vessels pulsed heavily. She could have sworn she felt them swirling and becoming red around the corners of her eyes, but she kept her voice even. "Did her and her new friend go into that room?" Tasha asked, bringing her hand up and pointing at the last room on the right. All the women were now silent.

Tasha marched down the hall, pushed wide open the door that was locked this morning, and released a feral scream.

"WHERE ARE YOU GOING?!" Tina asked Tasha.

"Anywhere but here."

Not bothering to stop stuffing clothes into her duffel bag to look at her older sister, Tasha looked around the room one last time before calling a ride share to meet her at the assigned block in their neighborhood. They both heard the kids come in with their younger sister, Trisha. Seeing her nephews after they finished school used to be the highlight of her day, but Tasha couldn't bring herself to look at them now.

"Mama! Mama! Why Titi mad?"

Trisha scooped up her little one and stared into the room. "It happened again?"

Tina answered, "Yeah. But this time she say she leaving."

Tasha whipped her head at the two of them before either could speak again. "I am done with this shit! I put two locks on my door and a new deadbolt, but it still ain't enough to keep out a crackhead!"

Tina rushed to her side and slapped Tasha across her face. "Watch your mouth! That's yo mama you talking about, little girl!"

Feeling the harsh sting from her sister's hand was nothing compared to the truth of what she just said. Rubbing her cheek, Tasha nodded her head quickly before going back to packing. "Yeah, you right. But as far as I know now, that person is also the bitch that sold all the photography gear that I scrapped and saved up for over the last three years. And she can kiss my ass!"

Slinging her duffel bags over her shoulder and pulling her headphones over her head, Tasha shouted again as she walked past Trisha and her now crying nephew, "Tell her when I see her again, it's on site! I mean that this time, Trish."

Before Tasha could press play on her phone, she heard her little sister suck in her teeth. "Now who's gonna watch the boys for me this weekend?"

Whirling around on her heel, almost falling and dropping her duffle bags, Tasha locked eyes with her little sister. "That's all you're worried about right now?!" she yelled in disbelief.

"Stop all that yelling in this house before someone call the po pos!"

Tasha looked at her older sister and cackled, "You know damn well no city dog is coming out here at night! Miss me with that bullshit!" Turning her attention back to Trisha, Tasha sneered. "If it's a babysitter you need, try calling one of the dudes that helped you make those babies! They oughta be good for something besides skeeting in and sliding out of ya!"

She didn't hear what either of them were saying as she finally pressed play and turned up the volume on her headphones while going outside to wait on the ride share.

Chapter Two
The Last Last Time

Jerome

"Okay, that wasn't half bad. Let's clean it up and take it from the top." Jerome waited for the track to begin again as he looked over his lyrics in his notebook.

Just cause we all sinners, don't mean we gotta keep sinning.
Doing anything for the gram—anything for the bag—ain't how
you win.
Give it up to the OG and let him see you through!

His boy Mitch had come through with finding him a studio, and Jerome did not want to waste a minute of the time that he had paid in full for the next two days. Finding his zone and finally being able to speak his purpose into existence was the greatest feeling. The time passed, and before he knew it, it was nearing midnight.

"Alright man, I know you ain't got no one at home waiting on you, but I do. And she fo sho the jealous type."

The sound crew chuckled as Jerome sheepishly took off his headphones. "I'm sorry for keeping y'all so late. It's just I only have this weekend to get this LP done." *Before Senior comes back from his workshop . . .*

"It's cool, just don't make it a habit. Anyway, four tracks in one day? That's gotta be a new record up in here! Let's listen to these in the morning before we work on getting them to the sound masters tomorrow."

"Same time?" Jerome confirmed.

"Fo sho man!"

Jerome looked around at the sound booth one last time before letting himself out. As he walked to his car, Jerome thought he saw one of the female volunteers from church leaving the twenty-four-hour diner. Just as he was about to jog forward, the woman turned around and he stopped. It was one of the chicks from the other night at the gentlemen's club. Even from where he stood, Jerome could see that she was in a bad way. She pulled a napkin out of her take away bag and wiped her face before sitting on a bench. Throwing the tissue back into the bag, she then took out her drink and sipped it slowly with her eyes closed.

He wanted to go to her, just to see if she was alright. *A sister shouldn't be out in these streets alone. It ain't safe.* His phone beeped, taking his attention away from her. He looked down and grabbed his phone from his jean pocket. Then Jerome looked back toward the bench, but the woman that had been there was gone.

TASHA

This is what you get for trying to talk big with ya friends. Tasha finished her drink while walking back to the hotel. She had paid for three days and almost said a prayer of gratitude when the card went through with no issues.

First thing Monday, I'mma call Alexa and Rachel to sign the lease.

There was no way she was going back to that house. Feeling her already-puffy eyes swell again from another familiar family betrayal, Tasha swore it would be the last.

No matter what. I'm never going back to live with them again. I'll work the truck day and night if I have to!

Being alone in the hotel and not having to worry about hearing kids playing or having someone knock on her door late at night felt strange.

It's strange, but it ain't like I can't get used to it.

She called The Photo Shop to make sure her new gear would be available for pickup tomorrow, and after getting confirmation that she could pick up her equipment first thing in the morning, Tasha eased into the lavender scented bed and drifted off to sleep.

PATRICK AND HIS BOYS were hanging outside next to the food court at the mall, and he squinted when he saw a chick go into The Photo Shop at the far end of the mall.

She kinda cute, I guess. If you like 'em fluffy, he thought.

Then he thought back to the night the crew got together to celebrate Wyatt's bachelor party at Bottom's Up. He stood up from the food court benches and started fuming. *That bitch! She threatened to call the cops on me?! Just who is she, anyway?*

"Y'all remember those chicks from BU?" he asked.

His boys laughed before Mitch spoke. "Yeah, I remember you and Chuck almost going to jail that night too," he joked, making Patrick deepen his frown.

"Whatever man, that bitch wasn't gonna call nobody," Patrick said, waving his hand in the air.

This time their boy Chuck joined in the chat. "I don't know man. After you left, some of the fellas filled me in about the girl that runs the truck out there. Apparently, she got some bite to her bark. Good thing choir boy was there to smooth things over."

"What you mean?" Patrick asked.

Chuck looked at him as he sipped his lemonade. "A few weeks after the truck got there, someone tried to jack her equipment. They say that homegirl flipped and smashed all his windows before calling the cops to report it."

"She did WHAT? Why she ain't locked up?! Mitch asked.

"By the time the cops showed up, all her equipment was brought back, and she code-switched on the po pos, said she didn't see who did it, that it must've been an 'isolated incident.' Apparently, she found out from a few dancers that the dude had priors and used that to get her stuff back."

"Damn!" Hearing this news only pissed Patrick off more. "Does anyone know her? Is she from 'round here?" he questioned.

Mitch answered for him, "That's the real tricky part. She a Daye girl. The quiet one that wanted to go to college and shit."

Chuck nodded. "Yeah, I remember them. My boys ran train on one of them girls back in the day. We ain't even know about her until we saw her walk the stage at y'all's high school graduation. She must have lived on school grounds or some shit to stay hidden like that."

Patrick sneered as he saw the girl in question walk out of The Photo Shop with two black bags, beaming like she won the lottery.

"Whatever. She must not be shit if she gotta work a food truck to pay rent."

TASHA

"Is this seriously all you have, Tash?" Rachel asked for the second time that day.

Throwing the last duffel bag in the corner of her new room and trying not to think of what went down at her family's place last week, Tasha forced out a laugh. "What can I say? I travel light."

Alexa walked in and smiled. "I'm just glad that you agreed to move in with us! Did you call the church already?" she questioned eagerly.

"Of course I did! And we were able to work out a schedule for me to tutor the kids in the afternoons."

Alexa and Rachel both clapped excitedly. "I'm so happy! Now you'll be able to save so you can finally travel like you are always talking about," Rachel reminded her.

Tasha's forced smile was going to give her a headache just thinking of how wrong her well-intentioned friend was about her future plans. *My ass will be eating food truck leftovers for weeks to cover just the deposit to this joint.*

Though the more she took in her new surroundings, Tasha couldn't even be mad. She now lived in a gated community! Her room even had its own private bathroom, which was something she could only dream about having back home. With a nice ceiling fan and an enormous window that overlooked a man-made lake, Tasha had a place that she was happy to call home. Looking at her two friends, Tasha felt her heart get lighter and heavier at the same time.

"Thank you. Seriously, I really needed to move out. Maybe in a few months, I can even start looking into going back to college." *Especially now that I'm not paying a mortgage to support folks who don't give a shit about me . . .*

Rachel and Alexa looked at one another before bringing Tasha in for a hug. "You know you're our A-1 since day one, sis!" Alexa shouted.

"Yeah, yeah. Let me up for air y'all! Dang!" Tasha joked as the two girls squeezed her in their three-way hug. Their giggles filled the room along with Tasha's heart.

JEROME

"Jerome, did you clean out that old nursery? The new tutor will start working there today," Senior, Jerome's daddy, reminded him for the third time that day.

"Yes, sir."

"Are you sure? How did you find the time? What, with all your staying out late these days?"

I knew he would find out about me going to the club.

Jerome stopped, looking over his notes from the jamboree as he stared up at his father. "I cleaned it before going out, sir," he told him matter-of-factly.

"Are you not even ashamed of being out at that hour? Only folks out at that time of night are the devil's children and his playthings! You know that, don't ya boy?!"

I should've waited for him to leave first before coming in today. "Sir, I went out with friends to celebrate a marital union. That's all."

"Are you sure that's all you did?"

Not this again! Is he ever gonna let up on—

"Now that you have been living on your own for some time, you may be thinking of giving into the pleasures that the flesh provides . . ."

Jerome could go the rest of his life without hearing more talks like this from Senior. Lucky for him, the creaking of the church doors opening, as well as footsteps echoing from down the halls, put an end to what was sure to be another uncomfortable lecture.

"We'll continue this conversation later," Senior told him sternly.

Jerome prayed they would not see each other for the rest of the day.

"Hello? Is anyone here?" A woman called out into the building.

Seeing his father practically sprint down the hall almost made Jerome follow him, but he remained seated and went back to his notes. Besides, Jerome knew he could hear whatever they talked about just fine from his office.

"Welcome to Christ's Corner! Mrs..." Senior trailed off and waited for the woman to answer.

"Ms. Daye. Tasha Daye," she finished.

For a few seconds Jerome didn't hear anyone speak, he only heard the sound of shoes slapping against the tile floor.

"Sir, are you okay?" he heard the woman ask his father.

Jerome was about to stand, growing concerned, until he heard a cough and some noncoherent sounds from Senior. Luckily, the new tutor could make out whatever his father had asked her. "That is correct. My last name is Daye. With an 'e' at the end."

"Yes, of course. I should have remembered that from your resume."

"It's not a problem, sir. We only spoke once briefly over the phone."

Hearing his father's egotistical laughter made Jerome roll his eyes. "And they say the youth today have no manners! Please, call me Jerome," he instructed her.

"Would Mr. Jerome be alright? I don't want to be disrespectful to my elders."

Jerome slipped on his headphones to tune out the rest of their conversation. Pulling out his notebook, he found himself inspired to write a few bars for a new song. There was no telling when he would find time to go back to the studio to bang out his new tracks, but he wanted to have material ready, just in case. Before he knew it, he had a steady hook and was mid-first verse writing 'Phony Prophets' before a bible was dropped over his notebook.

"Jerome Earl Grant Junior! Answer when I call you boy!"

Snatching out his headphones, Jerome looked up at his father and noticed that he was not alone. The woman from the food truck last week was by his side, and her eyes were wide in shock at the sight of him.

TASHA

I knew this gig was gonna be too good to be true!

First, the pastor started acting weird after hearing her last name and now this mess? Tasha groaned inwardly as she locked eyes with one of the creeps from the club. *It's always the quiet ones*, she thought as she tried to remind herself not to cuss inside a church.

"This here is the new tutor, Ms. Daye. Ms. Daye, this is my son, Jerome."

Watching him stand, Tasha got a glimpse of what he was writing. *Working on bars? In the Lord's house, of all places?* she wondered. *They probably corny as hell.*

Smiling to keep herself from snorting out loud, Tasha extended a hand towards Jerome. "It's nice to meet you, Jerome," she replied with years of false cheerfulness from working in retail.

"Y-you as well, Ms. Daye." His hands were clammy, and his eyes didn't reach hers as he shook her hand.

Yep, he remembers me. But I can't let that stop me from taking this job, she reminded herself.

"So, Mr. Jerome, who will I report to from now on?" she asked the pastor, remembering to throw him an encouraging smile.

"My wife wants me home at a respectful hour these days, so please check in with my son before and after your shifts. Today you have only two students, but once word gets out that we have a new tutor, that number will increase," he explained.

"I understand. And thank you for this opportunity," she replied dutifully.

"It is my pleasure! Ms. Daye, can we expect to see you more at Christ's Corner?"

I knew this shit was coming! Ugh, like I would want to spend my free time in this place. Keeping her stank face out of range and practicing the lie that she had prepared for this part of the conversation, Tasha sweetly replied, "I have a few volunteer hours with a local business to complete, but I should be able to make more time for one of your sermons soon, Mr. Jerome."

Watching the older man beam told her he bought her line.

"That is good to hear! Have a great first day, Ms. Daye."

Hearing him chuckle at that last sentence made Tasha want to leave in the worst way, so instead she thought about not having to lock her room door in hopes of keeping people out of her space as she giggled along with the older man.

"Jerome, make sure that Ms. Daye has everything she needs."

Tasha watched as his son nodded.

"I will sir," Jerome replied weakly.

God! Could he sound any more pathetic?!

As Mr. Jerome left the small office, Tasha noticed Jerome trying not to stare at her. *Let's train him now, because I need this gig to work.*

Turning her attention to him, Tasha gave him a frosty smile before speaking, "I already have everything that I need. Please use the office phone to let me know when the students arrive, and I'll stop by to leave any notes that I may have on your desk before leaving for the evening. Thank you."

She then turned to leave the office, not bothering to wait for his reply.

EVELYN

As she finished fixing Jerome's plate, Evelyn stared at all the leftovers that she had to put away. The house just wasn't the same without her children in it, and Evelyn fought back tears as she thought of them both being gone.

Eva's been gone for so long now . . . and Jerome finally left. What will I do with myself? she wondered hopelessly.

Quietly, Evelyn began putting the leftover food into individual containers and writing the day's date on them as she placed them all into the fridge. Hearing the front door unlock, her heart dropped as she fixed her face for a second time and went to greet her husband.

"My goodness, woman! It smells good in here, as always." He kissed her cheek as she took his coat. Evelyn made quick work of organizing his shoes with the others after he kicked them off and headed into the kitchen. "I was against it at first, but I think you may have been right about the church hiring a tutor for the kids, Evelyn," Jerome commented loudly.

That got her attention as she went to join him in the kitchen. Jerome sat down and waited as Evelyn served his meal and poured him a glass of cold water. He began to enjoy his meal while telling Evelyn more about his day before she could join him at the table.

"I was real smart and called up that new law firm to find someone for half the price, just like those uppity white folks in the neighborhood do. She's a woman, but I guess that's better. Should be good with the kids, even if she ain't married yet," Jerome explained as Evelyn tried not to let her excitement show.

He hired an unmarried woman? she thought excitedly. Choosing her words carefully, Evelyn first praised him for taking her advice, "I'm so happy for you. This could help you reach the younger generation in your future sermons." Seeing him nod as he continued eating, Evelyn went on with her next question. "You said that the woman is not married? Maybe her husband passed away?"

Jerome waved his hand in her face as he took a gulp of his water. "She looked too young to be widowed already, but you know it's considered impolite to ask those kinds of things nowadays. That's why I prefer to work with men! We can talk more freely without our little feelings getting in the way."

Evelyn closed her eyes at his last senseless statement and softened her jaw by choosing to smile at her husband from across their dining room table. They ate the rest of the meal in silence. Jerome got up and went to shower as Evelyn began clearing the table and washing the last of the dishes left in the sink.

Thinking about what her husband shared with her, Evelyn couldn't help but wonder if maybe this new tutor would get along with her son. *It would be nice for him to have someone to see outside of church,* she thought as she stared out at the deep violet sky from her small kitchen window. *Maybe someday we could welcome the sound of little ones in this house again.*

As she thought of her oldest child and how she was now missing out on seeing her only grandchild grow up, Evelyn silently let the tears fall down her cheeks.

Chapter Three

Scrapes and Sweet New Beginnings

Jerome

Two weeks had gone by, and just as his daddy predicted, Tasha Daye's schedule increased. She'd gone from having two shy students to eight curious ones, and Jerome seemed to spend more of his time during the day working as her assistant than as a youth minister.

"I understand Mrs. Williams, but right now, our tutor is only available for a limited time during the week. If you wish to reserve time for her to tutor your daughter, please leave a message at the number that we have provided, and she will contact you directly." Jerome repeated the number to the older woman and as he ended the call, he thought about not putting the phone back on its receiver so he could finally have a little peace. *That was the fourth parent today calling to book a tutoring session for their child,* he noted.

She was great with the kids, Jerome had to admit that. If he had had a teacher like her in school, he would have been just as eager to learn as the kids from the church are when they were in the office with Tasha. She insisted on leaving the door open during all of her lessons, and Jerome could hear her laugh every so often. Her voice ranged through clear, never raised, but stern when necessary.

Jerome wanted to get a peek into Tasha's current lesson, so he left his office and walked down the hall after finishing his expense report for the jamboree in the next few weeks. When he turned the corner, he didn't see anyone sitting at her desk. Instead, there was a large whiteboard against the left wall with the words, 'Why Change Should not be up for Debate' written in purple ink. Tasha was watching intently as Patricia, whose family was new to the congregation, was writing something down. Tasha hid a laugh behind her lips with her hands before walking up to the younger girl.

"Okay! Now we're getting somewhere. I know what you are saying, but how can we make it sharp?" she asked.

Patricia must've looked just as confused as Jerome was, because Tasha explained further, "We know your opinion on this political debate and why, but I need an example to strengthen your stance. Make it relevant and be mindful of your grammar," she instructed gently. "Remember, if you resort to using slang, the house wins. And we have enough men in the house as it is."

Patricia must have found that last line funny, as she giggled before going to write on the whiteboard again. Tasha was soon laughing too as she read what the younger girl had written for her last sentence.

"What you said - about having enough men in the house - helped me think of what I wanted to say," the girl mumbled.

Tasha took out a blue dry-erase marker, and Patricia's eyes widened. *What is she gonna do?* Jerome wondered to himself. He watched on as Tasha surveyed the sentence that Patricia wrote, and her smile left him feeling stupid. She then took the marker and drew what looked like dancing stars on the whiteboard, causing both of them to break out into more giggles.

"Outstanding work, Patricia! Fantastic use of heteronyms in the last sentence. Not gonna lie, you had me a little worried in the first half though, but ya pulled through!" Tasha praised the younger girl, making her cheeks redden just enough for Jerome to see from the room's entrance.

They then high fived one another before the buzzer on Tasha's desk went off. Patricia grabbed her backpack and notebook as Tasha called out to her while taking a screenshot of what they had written on the whiteboard.

"I'll send you this pic so you can finish up the rest of your essay. And I want to see an email of what you have written no later than Friday morning, cool?" she confirmed.

Patricia nodded gleefully. "Okay, Ms. Tasha. See you later!"

The girl almost bumped into Jerome on her way out of the room. As he was walking back to his office, he heard Tasha's voice. "Are you in need of English lessons as well? Or just a reminder in good manners?"

Jerome froze.

Turning around, he saw her leaning against the door frame, her hair now down and cascading around her face. Tasha's eyes looked softer somehow to Jerome, with her mid-length twists framing her full cheeks.

"Are you going to continue to stare at me like a lost dog or answer my question?" she asked.

For the last few weeks, Jerome would usually let her sly remarks fall by the wayside, but after having to field calls for her all day instead of spending more time on his own tasks, he was done with Tasha being short with him. Cautiously, Jerome entered the room, walked up to her, and sat down across from her desk.

"I meant no disrespect by looking in on your lesson, Ms. Tasha—"

"Daye. Call me Ms. Daye," she interrupted.

Sighing, Jerome continued, "I just don't understand why you are so cold toward me. What have I done to warrant this treatment?" he asked sincerely.

Tasha looked at him before she turned away to wipe down the whiteboard and finally sat at her desk. She then looked at her phone before speaking. "I know you remember me from that night at my other job. And I don't need any problems with this one. My homegirl recommended me for this position, and I want to do well for her sake. The only way I can think of to keep order here is by putting—and keeping—you on a short leash."

Jerome blinked several times before he addressed all that she shared with him. "So, because of the actions of a few, you are keeping me at arm's length?" he confirmed.

Tasha nodded, and he laughed.

"What's so funny about that?" she snapped, looking straight at him.

Jerome stopped laughing as he explained, "Women get mad when men do stuff like that, and here you are, treating me so rudely. Do you not see the double standard in your actions?"

TASHA STARED AT HIM for several beats before her phone buzzed. Looking down at the phone's screen, she picked it up and began typing as she spoke again, "I hope you remember that PSA the next time you hang out with ya little friends. Please share your new findings with them at y'all next Fried Fish Fridays. You can leave now."

Jerome looked taken aback. *Just who was this woman?* he wondered.

Getting up, Jerome looked on as she finished typing on her phone and stared up at him. She then picked up a clipboard and studied it before looking at him again. "Did you need something else, Jerome?" she asked evenly.

This time Jerome didn't hide his annoyance. Frowning, he asked Tasha, "How do you do that?"

Her eyes squinted as she asked him directly, "Do what, exactly?"

Jerome sighed heavily before continuing, "How can you be so great with students and treat me like something you stepped in? I have been nothing but respectful toward you, but you speak to me as if I am some . . . some . . ."

Tasha put down the clipboard in her hand and crossed her arms over her chest. "Some what, Jerome? Some horny guy that refuses to take no for an answer, so he feels the need to resort to manhandling women to take what he wants? Some drunk that thinks women are beneath him, especially those that work at a gentlemen's club? Some what, Jerome? Please enlighten me as to where to group you in the future, so I don't have to give you any more of my time."

He had never heard a woman speak so brazenly inside a church before, and Jerome was about to remind Tasha just where she was, but her next student had walked into the room.

"Hi Ms. Tasha! I have my homework ready for you to look at like you asked."

Jerome almost did a double take as he watched Tasha's face soften when she stood up to greet James, a high school sophomore and the youngest son of one of the deacons at the church. She went over to the young boy, and the two fist bumped before James looked at Jerome.

"Why is he here, Ms. Tasha? Are you in trouble?" the boy teased as Tasha giggled.

"I don't know why he is still here. Maybe you can ask him to tell you."

Jerome was left speechless as the two of them looked at him expectedly, and he slowly shook his head. "I-I was just checking in with Ms. Ta—Daye, Ms. Daye, about her schedule. We can finish discussing it at another time," Jerome sputtered out as he made his way out of the small office.

Tasha called out to him, "There is no need to discuss it any further, but thank you for stopping by. I'm glad we finally got to chat."

Jerome felt like his entire face was on fire as he watched Tasha begin her lesson with James. *Why does she feel the need to treat me this way?* he thought furiously. Jerome could hear his office phone ringing, and he jogged to answer it.

"Hello Jerome! I wanted to know when Ms. Daye would be free to tutor Keisha? Carmichael's girl had nothing but sweet things to say about her, and our baby could use a little extra help in her classes . . ."

Jerome closed his eyes as he relayed the same message again to the parent on the end of the line. Once the call was done, he puckered his lips together before disconnecting the receiver cord from the wall and reclining into his desk.

TASHA

Three weeks into working her new job, Tasha was ecstatic. Her students were really sweet; they mostly lacked confidence in their abilities, so Tasha showered them with praise during their lessons. After her chat with Jerome the week before, she noticed a change in his demeanor. No longer did she find notes on her desk from parents that wanted to schedule tutoring sessions with her. Instead, there was a new bulletin board just outside Tasha's door. It listed her available schedule as well as her contact number.

Nice work, Jerome, she thought as she entered her room.

One of her favorite students, Patricia, walked in soon after she did, and from the look of the younger girl, Tasha could tell that it was going to be a long lesson. Her school uniform was torn around the collar and covered in what looked like some sort of black markings. Once Tasha saw Patricia's face up close, she went into her top drawer and took out the first aid kit.

Walking over to Patricia, Tasha sat in the chair closest to the desk and motioned for Patricia to sit next to her. The younger girl dragged the chair toward Tasha, who then opened the kit and began cleaning the scratches around Patricia's eye and the cut on her upper lip.

"So . . . do you want to talk about it, or do you want me to just teach and mind my business?" Tasha asked her flatly.

Patricia looked up at her and squinted her eyes. "You ain't like other teachers, Ms. Tasha."

Tasha feigned shock as she gasped loudly. "Really?! I guess that's because I'm technically just a tutor, not a teacher, uh?"

Patricia giggled and then tensed up for a second as Tasha applied a light dab of the ointment to her bruises. "I guess we can do both," Patricia mumbled.

Tasha nodded. "Cool. Start when you're ready, and I will listen. No judgment here."

She pointed to the "Tutor Rules Chart" on her desk, and Patricia sighed as she recited the second rule: "This space is a judge-free zone, so do your best to not judge me and I will do the same."

Satisfied with her response and putting a bandaid over the largest of the bruises, the one near Patricia's left eye, Tasha closed up the first aid kit and waited patiently for Patricia to begin.

"Okay, so I have this friend at school who likes this boy, right? She asked me what I thought of him, and I told her he was boring and not as smart as he wants people to think he is. She got mad and stopped talking to me."

Tasha nodded as Patricia continued.

"Well, come lunchtime, some girl came to my table saying that I was talking smack about her brother. I was like, 'I don't even know you or your brother.' Then my friend said that I said he was stupid. So I stood up and told the girl that that's not true. What I said was he was boring. Then the girl got loud and called me . . ."

Tasha gently pressed on, "She called you what, Patricia?"

Tears formed in the young girl's eyes as she shouted, "She called me a closet licker!"

Seeing how upset the girl was, Tasha felt bad for having to ask, "What is a closet licker?"

As Patricia stared at her incredulously, Tasha chose then to remind her, "Look, I am much older than you and don't keep up with all the slang y'all be using these days, so I'm sorry, but I really don't know what that phrase means."

Tasha watched as Patricia cleared her throat to explain, "It's what we call girls that secretly like other girls, Ms. Tasha. A l-lesbian."

She put her hand on top of Patricia's as she spoke directly to her. "Okay, first things first. There is nothing wrong with being a lesbian, you got that?"

The girl's eyes widened as she nodded slowly at Tasha.

"And second, is that really what this fight was about?" she asked.

Patricia stared down at her hands. "Well, I don't know. I remember seeing my friend laugh with everyone else when that girl said that to me. I got angry and swung at her first and then the other girl started hitting me."

Damn. So her homegirl flipped and left her hanging, Tasha thought sadly. "So, you weren't angry about what the other girl said, but by what your friend did?" she clarified.

Patricia thought over what Tasha asked her and frowned. "Yeah!"

Tasha pressed on. "Why did that make you angry?"

"I thought she was my friend! And she just laughed when that girl made fun of me."

Tasha looked at Patricia as the girl realized what she said, and her eyes widened. Deciding that that was enough self-discovery for one day, Tasha stood up and went to the whiteboard to begin their English lesson.

THE TWO WORKED QUIETLY after their talk, as Tasha wrote a few example sentences onto the board. Then Tasha explained to Patricia that she was to read each sentence, find the errors, and then correct the mistakes within the sentences. Every few minutes, Tasha would feel Patricia's eyes on her, but she ignored it and continued instructing when necessary. Before the buzzer went off, signaling the end of their lesson, Patricia put down her marker and faced Tasha.

"Ms. Tasha?" Patricia whispered.

"Hmm?" Tasha said as she looked over the corrections Patricia made in the last sentence.

"Am I going to hell?"

The shock must've shown on Tasha's face, because Patricia quietly explained, "My mama said that girls that like girls won't go to heaven because it's a sin."

Feeling a slight stinging building behind her eyes, Tasha looked down at the younger girl. "Now, a disclaimer real quick. I am not the most religious person. I can't even tell you the difference between the New Testament or the Old one, okay?"

Patricia laughed, and seeing the girl's eyes light up tugged at Tasha's heartstrings.

"I say that to say this—I may not know much about the bible, but I doubt that the big OG in it would send someone as kind and clever as you to hell for not liking boys." Patricia looked at Tasha as she finished answering her question. "Since we are all supposed to be made in his image, why would he cast you out for being the way he made you?"

Before Patricia could say a word, there was a knock at the door. The two turned to see Jerome standing awkwardly in the frame.

"Patricia, your mama is waiting for you outside," he informed them quietly.

I just know you were eavesdropping again, Tasha thought as she narrowed her eyes his way.

The younger girl took out her phone and snapped pictures of the whiteboard before Tasha could. As she left the room, Tasha called out to her about the rest of their lesson and her homework, "Please send me those pictures Patricia! And be sure to finish the last three sentences before—"

Tasha's eyes went as wide as saucers as the young girl turned around and sprinted back toward her, wrapping her arms around her waist. "Thank you, Ms. Tasha," Patricia murmured into her chest.

Slowly, Tasha hugged her back, rocking them gently from side to side before Patricia broke their embrace and ran out of the room.

Umm, okay. I need something sweet before my next lesson, Tasha thought.

Going back to her desk to get a snack from the bottom drawer, she heard Jerome speak again, "James won't be in today. His daddy called earlier to let us know he broke his arm during JV football practice today and is at the hospital."

Hearing this news, Tasha sat down. "Thanks Jerome," she mumbled.

"Are you okay?" he asked her as he walked back into the room and sat down in the chair across from her.

I didn't think this job would have me wound up like this, Tasha admitted to herself.

"I think I'll leave early today, since my last student won't be coming in. Is that okay?"

He stared at her and nodded. "Yeah, but you haven't answered my question."

When she realized she hadn't, Tasha laughed softly. "You're right, I didn't. In that case, no, I'm not okay today," she admitted out loud.

Jerome stood up and looked at Tasha before he asked her another question. "Did you have lunch yet?"

She looked up at him and smiled.

INSTEAD OF LEAVING the church, Tasha found herself with Jerome in his office having the best lasagna casserole she'd ever tasted.

"I moved out years ago, but my mama still makes sure that I'm eating her food almost daily."

Tasha listened to him talk as she took another hearty bite of her meal. "Well, if you ever need help finishing leftovers as good as these again, please feel free to call me, okay?" she told him.

Tasha then stood up to take her plate into the kitchen area as Jerome reached out to take the plate from her. Their hands briefly touched, causing her to flinch. Tasha noticed the way his face fell, and she silently hoped that he would let what just happened go. The big OG must have been looking out for her as Jerome wordlessly left the room with the empty dishes. Hearing water running, Tasha wondered if she should leave.

The boy just shared his bomb ass lunch with you! It would be rude as hell to leave without at least saying thank you, Tasha reasoned. Willing herself to wait for him to re-enter the room, Tasha looked toward the door and watched as Jerome came back inside.

"I thought you would have left while I was away," he told her honestly.

Now feeling guilty as ever, Tasha chose her next words carefully. "I was going to, but it felt real impolite to leave without saying thank you for the meal. And . . . I also wanted to say that I'm sorry. I have been really rude to you these last few weeks." Tasha thought back to how harshly she had been speaking to Jerome since she started working at the church, and she winced. "It's just . . . this job is one that I really want to work out, and I thought you might try to use what you know about me to your advantage. I'm sorry."

Jerome looked at her and Tasha fidgeted around with her hands. When he grinned, Tasha felt an immense weight lifted from her shoulders.

"Thank you for telling me that. But to be honest, I don't know all that much about you, except what I hear you share with the kids in your lessons sometimes," he explained.

He really is naïve. Tasha thought. *It's kind of cute though.*

To complete her olive branch tour, Tasha met Jerome in the middle of his office and extended her right hand toward him. "Hello Jerome. My name's Tasha, but friends call me Tash." She smiled genuinely at him for the first time since working at Christ's Corner and found herself admiring the twinkle that now danced behind his warm brown eyes. They hadn't been this close before, so Tasha used this moment to take in more of his features. His skin was a deep, almost dark brown, which seemed to make his smile that much brighter.

"Nice to meet you, Tasha. I hope I can call you Tash someday."

The way his smooth and rich voice pronounced her nickname sounded too good to her ears.

Jerome

The last month had been full of some of the best days Jerome had ever had at Christ's Corner. More vendors returned his calls and donated either supplies or time to the jamboree that was scheduled to happen in two weeks. Senior even began coming in only once a week.

That left only him and Tasha alone inside the church for most days, except for the evening bible study classes he taught. She had apologized for being mean to him before, but there were still moments when Jerome could sense that Tasha was not all that at ease when alone with him.

He kept that in mind and did what he could to make her more comfortable. Little things, like not sitting in the seat closest to her in her office and sending her messages in between students to let her know if one would be late or absent for the day. Having a late lunch together became their new routine, and Jerome looked forward to sharing his meals with her. Going home for his weekly family dinners wasn't so bad now, as he would return all the Tupperware from the previous week back to his mother, clean and empty. Happy to see him eating well, Evelyn would quickly refill each container with more food for the next week. Having to talk to Senior was still hard, especially when Jerome had news to share about his sister.

But if this is necessary to keep the peace, then I can live with it, Jerome reminded himself.

With each meal together, he learned something new about Tasha, and Jerome wanted to keep learning more about her. Today they were having chicken and yellow rice, and Tasha was telling him about her favorite side job. "You really want to know how I got into photography?"

As Jerome nodded, Tasha closed her eyes before shaking her head. He could see her fighting a smile and that made him grin.

"I saw some sisters from out of town taking pictures at the park one day, and I had never seen anyone that looked like me holding a camera. After watching them for a bit, I built up some courage and asked them what they were doing. They told me they were traveling photographers on their way to an assignment. One of them let me hold her camera while the other took photos of me."

Jerome waited for Tasha to say more. When she didn't, he looked at her and sent a small smile her way.

"When they left and I went back to work, that moment was all I thought about that day. So after saving up for a few months, I treated myself to an old digital camera just to start playing around with and to at least learn the basics."

She went back to eating and Jerome tried to do the same. But for the past few days, he found himself taking in more than Tasha's company. She never wore anything revealing, but Jerome had to remind himself several times not to stare too long at her fuller figure or the lush twists that softly bounced behind her round face whenever Tasha stopped by his office to say hello in between seeing students.

A minute passed before he found himself asking another question. "So one photo of a stranger at a park led you to become a photographer?" Jerome asked as he took a sip of his lemonade.

Tasha peered at him over her bowl of food, and Jerome would have paid handsomely to know what she was thinking at that moment before she answered his question. "Well, stress led me to photography. My first client being a stranger at the park was just luck," she told him.

"What stress?" he wondered aloud and watched as Tasha tried not to laugh.

"Man, pick one! School, family, work. Everything was stressing me out. It got so bad that I started going to the park on my lunch breaks at a temp job that I had nearby, just to breathe."

Jerome wasn't sure if she was serious, but he went with his gut and picked one stressor that she listed off. "Family. How were they stressing you out?" He watched as her smile diminished halfway before she rolled her eyes in his direction.

"I'll tell you about that one some other time. For now, I think it's better to leave it out," Tasha told him as she went back to eating her lunch.

They were quiet for a few minutes before Jerome tried again. "Okay. What about school then?"

Tasha looked at him and smirked. "You are persistent. I can't decide if I like that the most or least about you."

Jerome chuckled. "And you are stalling."

Hearing her laugh the way she did with her students filled Jerome with a joy that he'd only felt when he was in the recording booth.

He briefly wondered what Tasha would think about his dreams of becoming a Christian rapper and decided immediately that she wouldn't judge him. That alone made him comfortable telling her about it someday.

She sucked in her teeth. "Fine big head, I'll tell you about that one. School was good until it wasn't. I went to Grover Community College for a few years, majoring in English before I had to drop out."

Jerome didn't want to pry, but he had to ask. "Why? Why did you leave before graduating?"

Looking him in the eye, Tasha replied sarcastically, "Family."

He said nothing after that, and the two finished their lunch in silence. Until his phone rang.

"I'll let you take that. Could be important," Tasha offered as she picked up their Tupperware and left his office.

Jerome hit send on his phone and spoke quickly. "Hey man!"

Mitch got straight to the point. "Yo, are you free tonight? Some of the fellas want to see if you can hang with them for a cypher that's happening in the next hour."

Dang! I'm supposed to stay here with Tasha until her last student leaves, Jerome remembered.

"If you can't, it's cool, but if you can come through, it'd be good for you to meet some of the other local rappers in the game."

Jerome looked at the clock in his office and answered, "Yeah, I can be there in half an hour. Is that cool?"

"That's what's up, PK! See ya then," Mitch answered before ending the call.

Now, how do I tell Tasha that I'll be gone for a while? A cypher shouldn't take that long, right?

As Jerome was placing the main phone line onto the automated voicemail night service, Tasha walked back into the office.

"Is everything alright?" she asked.

Seeing the slight concern in her eyes touched Jerome in a way he wasn't ready to admit yet, so he quickly grabbed his car keys as he explained to Tasha that he would be leaving the church. "A friend of mine asked me to help them with something. It's not too serious, but I probably won't be here when you finish seeing the last student tonight." He tried not to notice how her eyes fell to the floor and then quickly went back to his.

"Okay. I understand," Tasha said. Hearing the flatness in her voice compelled him to further explain himself. "He's helped me out before, and I feel like I gotta return the favor by showing up for him now. I know it's short notice, but I promise to come right back when I'm done, okay?"

Tasha nodded. "It's okay, really, I understand."

"Really? You're not mad?" he found himself asking.

"No, I'm not mad," she assured him.

The part of him that believed Tasha was trying not to feel some type of way about her response. Jerome was running out of time to meet Mitch at the studio, so he walked with Tasha back to her office and grabbed a sheet of paper. Jotting down the PIN, Jerome handed it to her.

"This is the security code to the building, just in case. Just turn off the lights and enter these numbers in the key box in Senior's office as you leave. You'll have five minutes to walk out after entering it though, so please make sure you have all your things with you when you're leaving, okay?" *Why do I feel so weird right now?*

"Just go already, big head! The sooner you leave, the sooner you can come back and lock up yourself, alright?" She then pushed him toward the entrance and waved as Jerome opened the double doors and left.

TWO HOURS LATER, JEROME was driving back to the church. The cypher went better than he'd hoped it would. A few of the guys laughed when they saw him, but Jerome had expected that before getting there. None of them expected him to match their flows during the cypher, and seeing the looks on their faces had Jerome in the zone faster than being alone in the booth ever did. He was so caught up in his rapper's delight high, Jerome didn't notice that Tasha's car was still in the parking lot. As he went to unlock the church doors to finish his class notes for tomorrow's bible study, Jerome had to step back quickly as the doors opened.

Tasha stared at him, and he couldn't make out the look on her face. It wasn't until he heard the background music from the cypher that he was in earlier that he realized why she was still at the church. He followed the sound to the phone in her hand and looked her in the eye.

"I must admit, I didn't think your bars would be that good," she told him. He watched Tasha playback the live from the recording studio's social media feed.

"The first day that I started working here, I saw your scribbles in that notebook of yours at your desk," Tasha said to him as she let him walk inside and to his office.

"Why didn't you say anything?" Jerome asked.

It was her turn to look embarrassed. "Truthfully? I was more worried about you telling your daddy where we first met. And . . . I just thought your bars would be weak," she shrugged as she sat down in the nearest chair. "A homegirl from BU sent me this live invite, and imagine my surprise when I saw the artist JPK take the mic," she told him with a glint in her eye. "I thought I was going to be watching a car crash, but you held your own."

"So, you like my sound?" Jerome asked her tentatively.

Tasha scoffed before answering him. "You could use a little work, but overall you did your thing. Gotta give you props."

Jerome held Tasha's stare as she continued, "Please do not keep something like this from me again. If you have a chance to chase your dreams, I am the last person who would stand in your way. But just be honest with me in the future, okay?"

He then saw her fighting the corners of her lips from turning upward.

"So, you want to be a Christian rapper, uh?" she said before laughing out loud.

Jerome continued staring at her as Tasha quickly explained, "Please don't misunderstand. I'm not laughing at you. But Jerome! You really went to a trap house—in the South—and started rapping about how sinning ain't really winning? Really, big head?!"

Confused, Jerome asked, "Was that a bad thing?"

Tasha wiped the corners of her eyes as she looked up at Jerome again. "It could have been! If you were off beat for even a second, those dudes would have laughed you all the way out of town! Did you even know who some of those rappers were before tonight?"

He shook his head, and that only made Tasha laugh harder.

"Yeah, the OG fo sho has your back. I have no doubt about that now."

Jerome watched her laughing at what happened to him today and not at his dreams. It felt good to be around someone that didn't make him feel weird or fake about what he thought his calling was in this world. He smiled and tried to soak up the sounds of her laughter as if they were rays of sunshine from the most high's arrival. Soon she was able to get herself together and stood up to leave.

"For real though, I think you sounded good. You definitely stood out in this cypher."

Jerome looked up at Tasha as she paused in between the doorframe and grinned at him again. "Let me know if you need a photographer for your first album cover. I know someone that may be willing to shoot it with you for a good deal."

Jerome returned her grin. "Bet. I will let you know."

Chapter Four
Family Bounds

T*asha*
  "I'm happy that you like the headshots Jade, and I'm sure you're going to hear from the talent agency real soon!" Tasha said cheerfully into the end of her phone while still in bed.

After ending her morning call with a new client, an aspiring actress ready to make her move to the East Coast, Tasha looked around her room and sighed dreamily. She had gone on an equipment-cleaning spree the other night, and beside her nifty fifty lens, everything else was left out of the gear bag. Alexa had left Tasha a note reminding her that the truck was being inspected later in the week. She welcomed the thought of having a day off from The Fast Fix. Tasha looked forward to coming home in the late evening like normal folks for a change instead of creeping in just before the sun.

In the meantime, she had to get ready for work at Christ's Corner, so Tasha lazily got out of bed and walked to her bathroom to shower and get dressed. As she went to the kitchen to fix herself a nice bowl of oatmeal with blueberries, she beamed as she saw Rachel about to leave the apartment.

"I see you're enjoying some time off!" Rachel teased.

Tasha winked at her before answering cheerily, "I am! But don't tell my boss."

The two shared a giggle before Rachel left for work and Tasha enjoyed her breakfast.

AS WAS THEIR NEW TRADITION, Tasha and Jerome shared lunch in his office before her students started to show up for the day. Even the few questionable glances from Jerome as he talked about the upcoming fundraiser for the church couldn't stop her from enjoying the plate of food.

"This is the second year that I've been running the event, so I'm hoping it has a great turnout," Jerome finished confidently.

Tasha looked up at him and smiled pleasantly. "I'm sure it will be a hit! You've worked really hard on finding vendors as well as donations for this jamboree." Thinking back to him taking her small check earlier, the two laughed.

"Every bit helps, Tash."

She stopped laughing mid-sentence as he used her nickname for the first time. *I was wondering when he would try it out,* Tasha thought as she looked at him.

Jerome didn't appear to be nervous at all. In fact, he went on eating his lunch like nothing had happened, and she felt her admiration for him grow a bit.

Their lunch ended, but the surprises from Jerome didn't, as he reached over and picked up a pastel purple box from the top of his desk. "I wanted to say thank you for the other night," he explained as he opened the top of the box and lowered it so Tasha could get a peek at what it contained. When she saw the half dozen cupcakes inside, she almost broke out into a dance on the spot.

"Sir! Are those from Ms. SweeThangs?!" she asked excitedly.

Jerome's nose scrunched up as he grinned. "They are. I overheard you telling Jay-Jay that their cupcakes were 'hands down' the best in the county. So I made a trip there and picked up a few."

Tasha hadn't had Ms. SweeThangs Cupcakes since her birthday last year. Alexa and Rachel had driven her out to the beach to cheer her up after Tasha had gotten into a fight with Tina about her not helping pay the mortgage again. She had hoped they wouldn't bring up the fact that it was also her birthday, but they did on the way home from the beach when the two of them noticed that the shop was still open. The memory of spending time with her girls and trying those cupcakes for the first time on what she thought would be another awful day brought tears to her eyes.

"Thanks Jerome," she whispered.

He stared at her, and Tasha could see that he was trying to choose his next words carefully. "I've been wondering something, and I have to ask, but please don't be upset, okay?"

Tasha looked at the box of cupcakes before leveling her eyes back up at Jerome's. "What is it?"

"I know no one has it easy, but from what you told me about your upbringing, and from what I've heard . . ."

Tasha's eyes widened and Jerome cleared his throat. "I mean no disrespect, but with all that you seemed to have gone through, how do you still smile the way you do?" Jerome gently asked.

Too afraid of bawling her eyes out from answering his question, Tasha took a more playful route as she looked up at Jerome again and smirked.

"I said that you can ask me, not that I would answer," she teased.

Tasha noticed Jerome press his lips together, so she added, "I'll tell you someday, okay? Just not now."

Tasha knew that she probably wasn't making much sense to him, but Jerome didn't protest as he put down the Ms. SweeThangs box. Peering inside the box again, Tasha really did want to cry when she saw the one cupcake she had hoped would be in there. Reaching inside, she gently grabbed 'The New CBD', a dark chocolate cupcake with a caramel sea salt drizzle and a butter pecan filling. The name hinted at the cupcake having a bit of chemically-enticing oil in it, but surprisingly it didn't. Biting into it, Tasha would've sworn that it was even better than the first time she had tried the dessert. To be fair, her homegirls smashed the cupcake into her face after singing a tone deaf and hip hop inspired version of the birthday song to her. Tasha had liked what she could eat off her face afterwards.

Her toes wiggled a little as the sweet and tart notes of the cupcake hit her tongue, and Tasha thought her day couldn't get any better. She then nudged Jerome, who was still looking at her.

"You gotta have one! Seriously, these bad boys are so dang good!"

Laughing, Jerome sat the box down next to her. "Oh, I know just how good they are, believe me. I bought eight cupcakes. Mama and I tried two of them together yesterday. These here are all for you."

And just like that, her day was instantly better.

WITH HER LAST STUDENT leaving for the day, all Tasha wanted to do was say goodnight to Jerome and head on home to her best friends and her super comfy bed. But as she was about to leave her office, Tasha heard two voices down the hall. *I thought they canceled bible study for the night*, she wondered.

Tasha was about to put down her messenger bag and see who was in the hall just as the two figures saw her. She wished like hell that they hadn't.

"What are y'all doing here?" Tasha whispered harshly toward her two sisters.

Tina was the first to speak. "Well, it's good to see you too," she said with too much sarcasm in her voice for Tasha's liking.

"You really working here?" Trisha asked as she looked around the corridor, shaking her head.

I do not need this mess right now! "Look, my shift just ended, and I'm on my way home. More importantly, I am not in the mood for whatever you two want to drag me into."

Trisha opened her mouth to speak, but she wasn't quick enough, as Tasha continued, "I don't know how y'all found out where I was and I don't care. Just go," she said as she turned back around to turn off the room light.

"Tash! W-we get it, really, we do, but hear us out!" Tina shouted.

"I lost my job, and the boys miss you!" Trisha blurted out right after Tina, neither one of them bothering to use their inside voices.

I swear! Lord, why me?! Tasha thought as she marched toward the two women and dragged them inside her office.

"Do y'all have any decency! This is my place of work and y'all come to me with this bull?!" Tasha turned away from them and slowly rolled out the kink that was forming in the middle of her neck before she faced her sisters again. "What happened with your job this time, Trish?" she asked flatly. Tasha watched as her sister looked around the room and finally made herself comfortable in one of the student chairs.

"They let me go last week," Trisha said after what felt like minutes.

Both Tasha and Tina waited for their sister to share more information, and the longer it took for her to say anything, the more annoyed Tasha got.

Sighing, Trisha finally explained, "So things were going good—real good —with my boss. He called me into his office that Tuesday afternoon, and I thought I was finally gonna get promoted to supervisor or something. But then, when I went to see him, his wife was behind the desk instead and told me I no longer work there!"

Tina shook her head as Tasha looked at her little sister and pinched the bridge of her nose between her index finger and thumb. *I swear, Lord! When will she get it together?!*

Tasha wasted zero time, or pleasantries, while filling in the blanks of what Trisha was telling them. "Let me make sure I understand this.

You were sleeping with ANOTHER married man, right? His wife found out AGAIN, except this time you lost your job because of it. How am I doing so far, sis?" Tasha spat out.

"It was different this time! He said they was getting divorced . . ." Trisha trailed off as both Tina and Tasha stared at her like she was a three-headed duck.

"And you believed him, Trish? Did he even show you some separation papers?" Tina questioned.

Trisha glared at both of her sisters before crying out, "See! This why I didn't want to come here! Y'all stay judging me!"

Tasha rolled her eyes. "Ain't nobody judging you Trish, but you stay doing dumb shit! And for what? Do the sex really be that good?!"

Tina, seeing Trisha grab a few tissues from the box on Tasha's desk, jumped back into the conversation. "Anyway, since Trish ain't working right now, we could really use your help. So just come back home Tash."

Tasha looked between the two women quickly, blinking her eyes to make sure she wasn't having a waking nightmare. "I know I didn't just hear you right," she said in disbelief.

Tasha started pacing the floor in tight circles as she stared off at both of her sisters. "Do I look like a fucking workhorse to you two?!" she finally shouted.

Tina then marched up to Tasha, but as she brought her hand out to strike, Tasha raised her face. "I dare you to pull that stunt again. You'll be meeting Jesus in minutes." Tasha's voice was calm, but Tina must have felt the chill in the air all the same.

She looked on as her big sister slowly dropped her hand and took three steps back as Trisha pleaded, "Seriously though, Tasha—you ain't gonna come back home?!"

Tasha was quick with her reply, "I have a home and y'all are keeping me from being there right now with this bullshit."

Tina shook her head before turning around to leave. Tasha watched as her older sister rested her hand on Trisha's shoulder. "Let's go. She ain't gonna come."

Pushing her hand away, Trisha bolted out of the chair and looked between them, clearly tired of not getting her way. "Girl, you have got to let this pettiness go!" Tasha's eyes widened as her little sister went on, "You think that you the only person she ever stole from in that house? Well, ya ain't. And I'm tired of my babies asking when you gonna be coming back. Every family has issues, so just stop playing and come back home!"

Tasha took note of Trisha's chest rising and falling during her rant, and to stick the nail in the proverbial coffin, she brought her hands together and started clapping. "That was a lovely performance. Too bad it came with abso-fucking-lutely no logic and way too much of your self- serving agenda." Tasha saw Trisha's eyes harden and laughed.

"You know what, fine! Turn your back on your family, but remember as you walk these holy halls—God don't like ugly, Tash!" Trisha barked.

"And the last time I checked, He didn't seem too fond of pretty either," Tasha told her evenly.

Trisha finally got up to leave with Tina, but midway to the door, Tasha heard her stage whisper to Tina, "Who else is gonna accept her weird ass? Ain't blood supposed to be thicker than water?" she added while cutting her eyes back over to Tasha.

Tasha was done with their microaggressions and the conditional love they had for her. These two came back into her world like a hurricane, wrecking her otherwise peaceful and sweet day with their issues. Which is why she made sure they heard her yell out, "Me! I will accept ME! More than y'all ever even bothered to."

As they turned around to face Tasha, she couldn't help but to keep going. "And I wish you had half the sense that I do. Maybe then you would learn the full phrase to that tired-ass saying before you try to use it to get me to do what you want me to." Clearing her throat and adding in her full evening news reporter's voice, "The blood of the covenant is thicker than the water of the womb."

Trisha sucked in her teeth while glaring at Tasha. "You always think you're smarter than everyone! That's why Kitty lied to your teacher and took your scholarship money back in high school!" As the words left Trisha's mouth, Tina looked over at Trisha and then at Tasha. The sudden agitation on her face was obvious.

"What scholarship money? What are you talking about?" Tasha asked. A minor storm began to make its appearance behind her eyes, which were now zeroing in on her big sister.

Tina nervously giggled, "You know Trish don't be making any sense when she don't get her way. Just come back home girl." Trisha went back to where she was sitting before, but she wouldn't look Tasha in her eyes.

Tasha asked again, "What scholarship money? When I was accepted into Benton University and went to see financial aid, I was told that I no longer had any scholarship funds."

Neither of her sisters would look at her and Tasha could feel the storm reaching the pit of her stomach.

"I always thought that they made a mistake, since I knew my English teacher submitted my senior essay. I still have copies of each of the scholarship essays that I submitted. One was even featured in the school paper! I-I thought . . ."

The currents of her storm comfortably settled down to the lower half of her limbs, and she felt her knees get weak. Tasha shrieked, "Tell me now!"

"Damnit Trish!" Tina looked at Tasha and started to explain, "All that happened in the past anyway, so it shouldn't even matter no more. It was during one of Kitty's relapses. She was trying to quit cold turkey, and your teacher called her on the house phone, saying that they needed her signature for your financial aid paperwork, since you were only seventeen and needed a parent's signature, or something like that. She was really trying to quit that time too! Anyway, she went to your school and met your homeroom teacher. They let her sign the funds over to another account. We was gonna surprise you with the funds later, but when the money came . . . well, Kitty did what she did and that was it."

Trisha and Tina waited for Tasha to say something. They waited for so long that eventually it was Trisha who spoke first.

"Tash? Girl, you scaring me. Say something."

"We? W-we?" Tasha asked looking up at Tina, face full of tears, hands shaking. "Whose bank account did the funds go to?"

Tina parted her lips to speak, and Tasha sprang into action. She wasted no time marching up to Tina, pressing her fingers hard into her sister's chest. "That was MY MONEY! My way out of this hellhole! You-you bitches had no right!"

Trisha quickly made her way between the two of them as she saw the unshed tears in Tasha's eyes.

"I had to swallow the last of my pride and register to take classes at Grove Community College, while everyone else left this fucked up place!"

With Tasha's attention on Trisha, Tina tried to make a run for the door but wasn't fast enough as Tasha pushed Trisha aside and yanked hard onto the back of Tina's braids. She continued yelling while looking down at her older sister, hands shaking and ready to strike if Tina even did so much as breathe wrong.

"For nights I cried myself to sleep in that shitty house! Made myself sick wondering what I did wrong!"

Tina's eyes were wide as she looked around quickly for a way from Tasha. "Tash, it wasn't like that! We was—"

"Y'ALL STOLE MY FUTURE!" Finally tired of ignoring the burning sensation in her hands and ready to lay them to rest on Tina's face, Tasha winded her right hand back but soon felt a larger one grasp it.

Tasha's head throbbed without mercy as the chance to inflict the pain she was due to deliver to Tina was taken away. She watched through blurry eyes as Tina scurried away from her and out the office door.

"Tash, that's enough."

Hearing Jerome's voice over her wounded heart was too much to bear. Crumbling into his embrace, Tasha felt the fight in her wash away, leaving nothing but hurt in its aftermath. She heard him speak again, but before she could make out what he was saying or to whom, darkness finally claimed her as Tasha went limp in his arms.

JEROME

He knew how bringing Tasha back to his place would look if anyone found out, but after getting her sisters to leave the church peacefully while he looked after Tasha, Jerome was exhausted and out of ideas. He didn't want to chance someone from the church's congregation seeing him bring a woman to his place in the middle of the night, so Jerome sat in his ride and hoped she'd wake up soon. Otherwise, they were going to sleep in this car together, which was almost just as bad, but what other choice did he have?

Trying to keep awake, Jerome turned on the radio and listened to the last of the Roddy RomStorm Love Hour. Just as the last song of the show began to play, he saw Tasha stirring awake. Turning off the radio, he waited for her to say something, but her stomach growled instead. She looked around, blinking her eyes as they adjusted to the lack of light.

"Where am I?" she asked groggily.

"Outside my apartment complex."

Seeing her arch an eyebrow in his direction, Jerome brought his hands out in front of her. "No ill intentions, but after . . . all that went down, and you passed out, I didn't know where else to go. Now that you're awake, I can take you home. Just tell me where."

He watched as Tasha looked out the window. "Nah, it's okay. I'll just text my roommates and crash here. If that's okay with you?"

Jerome nodded and watched as Tasha searched for her phone. Remembering that he placed all her belongings in the backseat, he reached for the bag behind him. "All your stuff is here." Handing Tasha her messenger bag, Jerome's fingers connected with hers, and the shock made him jerk his hand away. A small wave of embarrassment washed over him as Tasha glanced at him before looking away.

"Sorry."

"It's cool. You'd have to be crazy not to be a little cautious of me right now."

"Yeah, about what happened tonight . . ." Jerome started before looking at Tasha again. He saw her face fall and his need to comfort her almost made him reach out to touch her cheek. "I talked with your sisters, and they agreed to not come back to the church."

Tasha looked up at him and graced him with a small smile. "You didn't have to do that, but thank you."

"You're welcome. I couldn't help but overhear the conversation leading up to the, uh, altercation. Were those the parts of getting to know about your family that you left out when we talked before?"

He saw her nod and decided to not to ask any more questions. Jerome instead took off his seatbelt and let himself out of the car. He then walked over to the passenger side and opened Tasha's door. Leading the way to his apartment, Jerome tried not to let his nerves get the best of him about having a woman in his apartment for the first time. The keys jingled in his hand, and he could feel Tasha staring at his back as he finally unlocked and opened the door to his place.

Stepping in quietly, Jerome flicked on the living room light and placed his keys onto the wall hook as he took off his shoes.

"You know, this is much nicer than I thought it would be."

Turning to see Tasha gently push the door closed, he walked behind her to lock the deadbolt and continued to watch her take in his apartment. She then walked over to the couch and sat down.

"No huge TV or speaker system?"

Jerome wanted to join her on the couch, but he quickly decided that was a bad idea. Instead, he went to his small kitchenette and sat in the chair closest to the wall. "I'm mostly at work or my folks' house, so ain't none of that really important to have in here, far as I'm concerned," he answered.

"Not even a game console, though?" she wondered out loud.

Shifting a little in his seat, Jerome explained, "Well . . . we never had one of those coming up."

Tasha raised an eyebrow at him. "Wait a minute—you mean you never had a game console as a kid? What did y'all do for fun then?"

Jerome could see the genuine curiosity in her eyes, so he answered honestly, "We mostly played outside, me and my sister. She also taught me how to sign."

Tasha tilted her head, and when her eyes opened again, he knew where the conversation was going. For the first time in a long time, Jerome was at ease and ready to talk about her.

"Ah! I heard from Rachel that you have an older sister. What is her name?"

She really is interested in my sister? Not where she is or why she isn't in the church? Upon realizing this, Jerome felt a little silly being so far away from Tasha, but not sure how to make a move toward the couch. Fortunately for him, her stomach growled again and provided him with a perfect reason to get up. He then stood up and stretched as he walked into the small kitchen and took a peek inside the fridge.

"Her name is Eva." Seeing a few bottles of water and a white cardboard box, Jerome took them out and placed the pizza onto a plate. Hearing movement from the living room, he turned his head and saw Tasha getting up and heading his way. She took a bottle of water and twisted the top open, taking several hearty gulps while eyeing Jerome as he placed the pizza into the microwave.

"Is that dinner?"

The two shared a smile before the microwave beeped. Jerome took the pizzas out and sat the plate on the small table. Returning to his previous seat, Jerome looked at Tasha as she got comfortable in the opposite chair and stared deeply at the savory, all-meat supreme pizza slices in front of them.

"Tell me about her," Tasha said as she swiped a slice and bit into it.

Jerome watched her, this woman who had just learned of a deep betrayal from those closest to her, and if he hadn't been there to witness it himself, he would never have known anything had happened at all as she smiled while enjoying his day-old pizza.

How does she do that? With so many awful situations surrounding her, this woman was still able to find joy in even the smallest moments. Jerome thought she was just rude and combative when they first started working together at the church. But over the last few weeks, he could see that there was more to her than what he initially thought.

The kids at Christ's Corner loved having her as their tutor. She was patient and never looked frustrated with them while tutoring. If a parent was late to pick their kid up, Tasha would wait with her student and talk about school or what new hobbies they were into lately until their parent or guardian arrived to take them home. Jerome shamelessly eavesdropped on those conversations and found himself looking forward to getting a call from a parent telling him they were stuck in traffic and would be late picking up their child.

Even if it meant that she would have to stay at the church an hour later and rush home to get ready for her second job, Tasha never complained. Now Jerome wanted to really get to know Tasha Daye. *I guess if I want to know her, I have to tell her more about me.*

Taking a slice of pizza and looking across the table at Tasha, Jerome smiled as he thought about his sister. "Growing up, Eva and I were best friends. Honestly, for a few years, she was my only friend."

Tasha continued eating, so he went on, "I didn't know that there was anything different about my sister. Until the day of my first-grade graduation."

She finished her pizza and took a swig of her water before asking, "How was she different?"

"My sister is deaf. As a kid, I didn't know this was different. I just thought my sister talked with her hands a lot." He stared off for a moment, thinking of those days, playing tag with his sister and Eva teaching him to talk with her through pictures and using his hands. "I remember being so excited for everyone to meet my big sis. When my parents arrived, I could sense something was wrong, but as a kid, you don't know how to say that, right? So I went to Mama, gave her a hug. Then I started to talk to Eva the way we always did . . . and Senior grabbed my hands before whispering to Mama." He saw her piecing together what he just said, and her eyes darkened.

"He didn't want anyone to see you using sign language in public?"

Jerome nodded. "Come to find out that when my folks learned about Eva being deaf, my daddy thought it would be temporary. Mama eventually learned some ASL when Eva was four and about to begin pre-K."

Tasha bit her lip before she spoke again. "To grow up for that long and not have anyone to talk to . . .no one to understand you? That must have been hard as hell for your sister."

The two sat in silence for a minute before Jerome could take his eyes off of hers and continued, "I was born when Eva was three years old, so she was about ten or eleven then. I remember the look on her face that day when Senior grabbed my hands, and when I look back on that day, a part of me knew she would leave soon."

"When did she leave?" Tasha asked him gently.

Jerome's heart got heavy as he thought back to his fourteenth birthday. "Just before I started high school. She gave me all of her ASL books and made me promise to keep studying so I wouldn't forget what I'd learned. The next morning, I woke up to the sounds of Mama crying, and I saw that Eva wasn't in her room. We found out later on that she had faked my parents' signatures on some forms and applied for an early admission to a university in New York."

Tasha smiled, surprising Jerome with what she said next. "She must have been planning her getaway since your grade school graduation." Pushing the plate toward him, Tasha silently offered him the last piece of pizza. He took it and continued telling her the rest of the story before he lost his nerve.

"Eva hasn't left New York since. Even got married and had a kid of her own. I finally met them a few years ago when Mama and me took a quick trip there for her fiftieth birthday. Her daughter's name is Evelyn Mae, after Mama. The day we met her was the second time I had ever seen Mama cry."

Tasha's eyes filled with tears again and Jerome watched as she used the corners of her blouse to wipe them away.

"She sounds like someone I would love to meet someday," Tasha whispered before clearing her throat and looking at Jerome again. "So, did you keep your promise?"

Confused for a second, Jerome almost asked her what she meant, until he heard her squeal and bolt up from her chair.

"You did!" Tasha went to his small bookstand near his TV and picked up a recent copy of the *ASL Time's* magazine. She flipped through the pages, and seeing her eyes so full of wonder made Jerome's heart beat faster than it had all night.

"You don't think it's weird? What happened with my sister?" he asked.

Tasha looked at him and blinked several times before answering him with a question of her own, "Why would anyone think that's weird? Your sister is deaf. Okay? And?"

He sat down on the couch, and Tasha laughed before joining him.

"It's just... every time someone at the church would hear about what happened, they always try to say that it was the Lord's will or something. Like my sister being deaf was a trial sent to test Senior or something."

Tasha put down the magazine and looked him in the eye. "Maybe it was a test from the Lord. If so, in my humble opinion your Pops didn't pass."

Shock must've shown on his face, because Tasha started to explain what she meant. "We're supposed to 'honor' our father and mother, right? Well, what about you and your sister? Ain't your folks supposed to love y'all unconditionally too?"

Jerome thought about this as Tasha continued, "It seems like your mama was holding up on her end of the deal and your daddy fell short, that's all I'm saying. As you know by now, I have way too much experience in having a parent that is always failing at doing right by their kid." Tasha surprised him again that night when she took his hands into hers and looked at him sheepishly. "So, these hands can talk, uh? Teach me something then."

Blinking rapidly, Jerome pushed out the not-so-gentlemanly thoughts that came to his mind. Tasha must've picked on what was going on, as she quickly let go of his hands.

"You know what I mean! Get your head out of the gutter and teach me how to talk with my hands already, Rome!"

Hearing her new nickname for him, Jerome went into action as he turned to face Tasha a little more on the couch. "Okay. It's been some time since I've practiced, but we can start with the basics."

Jerome got so caught up in teaching Tasha the alphabet and a few other phrases in ASL, the two didn't realize how late it had gotten until Tasha yawned and Jerome glanced at the small clock next to his TV. "Dang, it's past midnight!"

"You right. I'm sorry to keep you up so late, "she apologized gently.

It was Jerome's turn to shake his head and laugh, "No worries, I really don't mind. But I have to go to bed soon, so . . ." Realizing that their sleeping arrangements hadn't been discussed beforehand, the two awkwardly stood up as Tasha took out her phone.

"Okay, I think it's best if I stay out here for the night," she suggested.

Jerome wanted to protest, but he remembered rushing out of his place late that day to go to the church on time and did not know what shape his bedroom was in. Nodding, he went to his linen closet and took out some spare pillows and bedding to give to Tasha. As he walked back into the living room, he saw her in the kitchen, toothbrush in hand as she brushed her teeth. Jerome placed the linens on the couch and waited for her to return.

"Sometimes when I didn't feel like going home after working the food truck late I'd treat myself to a night at a hotel," she explained as she rinsed out her toothbrush in the sink and set it on the countertop.

Was it really that bad at her home? Why did she stay for so long then? he wondered sadly.

Seeing her look at the linen and pillows that he brought out, Jerome moved on from his thoughts to talk about what his morning routine was like. "I usually start the day around seven, before driving to church at nine. So if you want to wake up around that time and get ready together, that's cool."

She shook her head, "I already set my alarm for five and planned on getting a ride share to the church to pick up my car."

He stared at her for a beat before asking the obvious question, "Why so early?"

"Do you really want me to answer that?"

Jerome nodded.

"Listen, I really appreciate you letting me stay here tonight, I do. But let's be real. If you and I walk out this door at the same time in the early morning... people will talk."

Hearing her explanation didn't bother Jerome. He hadn't thought about that when he'd suggested the plan to Tasha. However, there was a small part of him that was a little hurt by her reaction to his idea of starting the day off together.

"Tash, I don't mind. Really. We could wake up and go for breakfast at Wayward Waffles and be at the church before Senior gets there at ten."

His pride took an even bigger hit as she laughed out loud. Jerome watched as she shook her head and sat back down on the couch. "I'd love a hot plate of country fried chicken as much as the next girl, but Rome, be serious! You and I cannot be seen together in the morning."

Not bothering to hide his wounded ego, Jerome could hear the soft change in her tone as she continued talking.

"It's not that I wouldn't want to, you know, go have breakfast with you. But I have only been tutoring at the church for a month now. With the holidays coming up and all, I could really use the extra income. And I wouldn't want anyone to read more into our friendship than what is there, okay?"

Jerome understood what she was saying. He wasn't a complete dummy. But as he spent more time with Tasha, he had to admit that he wanted to see her more. The fact that she may not feel the same hurt. Wordlessly, he turned to go to his room and get ready for bed. Though before he made it to his door, Tasha called out to him. The sound of the new nickname from her mouth had him all too eager to turn around and look at her one last time for the night.

"How about I bring breakfast to you? Since my first tutoring session isn't until late tomorrow, I could go home, shower and then stop by Wayward Waffles and pick you up something? As a thank you for tonight, you know?"

The hopefulness that shined from her eyes left him grinning like the lovesick fool he was becoming.

"Okay."

TASHA

Trying to be as quiet as she could, Tasha freshened up and called a ride share to pick her up two blocks away from Jerome's place the next morning. When she arrived at her place, Tasha tried her best to be quiet as she unlocked the door, but she found herself face to face with her roommates. Alexa and Rachel both looked like little old ladies in their wraps and tattered sleepwear, as they wasted no time demanding to know where—and who—she was with last night.

"Y'all please. I just had a late night with a new friend and didn't want to disturb anyone by coming in here all kinds of late." She tried to explain.

"Okay . . ." Rachel began. "We appreciate that sis, but does this 'new friend' have a name?"

Alexa smirked as she followed up Rachel's question with one of her own, "And just where did you and this 'friend' spend the night, um?"

They ain't gonna let this go, Tasha realized.

She never was good at lying, so Tasha served the truth to them straight, no chaser, "I spent the night at Jerome's place."

Tasha would have sworn that she was talking to two teenagers instead of two grown women the way they both squealed and flailed around her.

"Tash! You finally tapping into ya babe baddie side, uh?!" Rachel teased.

"About time too!" Alexa chimed in. "But with the preacher's son? I don't know, sis. That could be messy . . ."

Tasha looked at them and shook her head. "It ain't like that at all, and y'all dead ass wrong for going there. I . . . I just got some bad news and was in a way afterwards. He made sure I was okay for the night. That's it."

The two now looked at Tasha, concern and worry showing on both of their faces. "Sis, what are you trying to keep from us?" Rachel gently asked her.

Dammit! I should've known they would get it out of me the first chance they got. Tasha sighed as she prepared herself for telling them about last night.

"Long story short. Tina and Trisha came by the church to talk me into coming back to the house. Trisha let it slip that both Tina and Kitty cleaned out all my scholarship money back in high school. So they were the real reason I never got to go to Benton like I wanted to."

She couldn't bring herself to tell them just how she took hearing that news, mainly out of embarrassment. But Alexa's now stoic face had Tasha a little worried. Her friend marched away from them, and Tasha thought they would finally let her go to her room without any more questions, until she saw Alexa again, wearing sneakers and wrapping a blue and yellow bandana over her head, making sure to tuck in her shoulder length locs.

"Wh-what are you doing, Alexa?" Rachel suddenly asked, a trace of panic in her voice.

"I'm going to beat thousands of dollars and a few years of heartbreak outta them hoes. You driving or nah Tash?" her friend flatly asked.

Rachel sprinted to the front door and grabbed Alexa's keys before she could get them from the key rack. "Babe, give me my keys!" Alexa shouted as Rachel slowly shook her head.

Tasha watched as Alexa then reached for the keys, only for Rachel to extend her arms out of reach. After a few missed swipes and seeing both Tasha and Rachel stare at her, Alexa finally gave up. "They robbed you, Tash!" her friend shouted angrily.

"Do you know how hard it was to watch you take classes at Grover? GROVER, sis?! And you then left there and worked like a dog for them so the bank wouldn't take that damn shack away. Why aren't you angry too, dammit?!" Alexa screamed as she got closer to Tasha's face.

Linking both of her hands into Alexa's and Rachel's, Tasha led them to the couch and they all sat down. "Trust, I was angry. Still am. Jerome saw me at the height of my rage, and if he hadn't been there last night . . . there ain't no telling where my ass would be right now." Looking up to the ceiling while blinking her eyes quickly, Tasha cleared her throat before looking Alexa in the eye. "So, I'm asking you to please let it go. What is it you always say, 'God wouldn't give you no more than you can handle?' Let me handle this, okay?"

"How are you going to do that though, Tash?" Rachel whispered.

Tasha looked at Rachel and sent her a soft smile. "First, I'm going to start by making sure not to be late for work today. And then I'm going to work on making peace with what they did."

Clearly, what she said was not what either of them expected to hear, as both girls stared at her. Alexa whistled slowly, "Just what is in the holy water at that church nowadays?"

They shared a laugh as Tasha gently pushed Alexa back into the plush couch. "I'm serious, so stop playing! I have to make peace with it, otherwise the rage and hurt that I felt last night will take over me again. After experiencing that once, I know I don't want to have that kind of experience again. Besides . . ." Tasha thought about what Jerome told her last night about his sister and parents. Blinking back fresh tears, she continued, "Every family has their issues. It's how you react to them that shapes you into the person you become. And I want better for myself than to end up like Kitty."

Her friends each perched their heads onto her shoulders, and Tasha finally let the tears that she had been holding back fall down her cheeks.

Alexa and Rachel wordlessly wiped the tears away and hugged Tasha tightly, as the trio remained on the couch.

Chapter Five

Petty Patrick, Reporting for Duty

Traffic was tight and noisy, but she got to Wayward Waffles in time to order two breakfast meals to go. While she waited for her order, Tasha stared out the window and thought about last night.

Why did they have to come to the church in the first place? she wondered.

Thinking about what happened between her and Tina, Tasha couldn't help but wonder if that wasn't Big G's doing up there, looking out for her. *Imagine if I had found out about what they did some place else?* Tasha shook that thought away and went back to checking her emails while waiting for her food. She saw a new message from Trixie, a dancer at Bottom's Up, and clicked on the text.

Hey!

Were you serious about doing a photoshoot for us girls sometime? The guy I normally go to just got locked up and I was hoping to get some new pics for my website this weekend.

Let me know!

Glee filled her whole body, starting from her toes, and by the time it reached the top of her head, Tasha had already sent off her reply to Trixie and couldn't stop beaming.

"Order 412!"

Hearing her take-out number, Tasha went to the counter to pick up her food and almost skipped out of the restaurant as she heard a ding on her phone.

Bet!

Me and some of the other girls will see you on Saturday at 4pm then.

The cash that Tasha was about to make this weekend would pay rent for the rest of the year, plus her leasing agreement for all of her new gear. Looking at herself in the mirror, she thought back to what Alexa asked her this morning and laughed.

There must be something in the water after all!

JEROME

As he reached over to turn off his alarm, Jerome lay in bed for a minute after it went off. Thinking about what happened at the church and his night with Tasha, it all felt like a dream. Before he went to brush his teeth and shower, he walked into the living room, hoping she would be there, but all he saw were the pillows and bedding that he had given her, folded and left on the end of the couch. *At least I know it really happened.*

It had felt good to look back on his time with Eva. Jerome remembered talking with Tasha last night and grinned as he thought about the way her face would scrunch up as she focused on watching his hands during their impromptu lesson. The squeals she let out when she would sign the right phrases still ranged in his mind. Jerome couldn't wait to see her again today, even if it meant that he would have to see more of Senior than he liked to; he didn't care.

Jerome was falling for Tasha, hard.

Once he stepped out of the shower and got dressed, Jerome went to pick up the linen and pillows from the living room. Seeing a note from a torn piece of paper fall from the top of the sheets, he read it and laughed out loud.

Felt like I was sleeping in Antarctica last night!
Just what do you have the A/C set to in this joint?
Anyway, text me when you read this and tell me what you want for
breakfast.
See you soon, big head.
-Tash

As Jerome sent Tasha his breakfast order by text, his phone chimed again with a new message.

God is my strength and power - 2 Samuel 22:33-35

Seeing the inspirational text from his mama and thinking of Eva, Jerome made a mental note to call his sister after work today and pressed "1" on his phone as he grabbed his car keys.

"What did I do to deserve a call from my baby on this fine day!" Evelyn singsonged into the receiver.

"Good morning to you too, Mama," Jerome said as he switched to his Bluetooth device in the car.

"Are you on your way to work? And did you eat breakfast?" she questioned. "You know your daddy won't be there until later in the morning," Evelyn reminded him.

That's why I'm going in now, Jerome thought as he slowed down at a four-way stop sign.

"Yes ma'am, I'm heading to church now. I'll be having breakfast with a friend in a bit," he told her.

"Oh, okay then, baby. You still coming over for dinner tonight?"

"Yes ma'am."

"Good! Then I can tell you and your daddy about my idea for the church's jamboree this Saturday. Do y'all still need volunteers?" she asked.

Jerome didn't get as many church members to sign up as he had originally hoped for, as he had spent the week avoiding Senior. Even going as far as to clean out the attic instead of working in the office when his father was at Christ's Corner preparing his sermon for the week. Instantly, he thought of asking Tasha to help him during the event and felt better. "I'll ask Tash if she is free to help for a bit," he said out loud.

Not a beat had passed before Evelyn spoke into the receiver, "Ah, I heard your daddy talk about this new tutor. Ms. Daye, is it?"

Jerome knew that tone from his mother all too well. And after Tasha dashed his hopes before he'd had time to fully express them, he found it a little funny that he was now about to do the same with her. "Yes Mama. The kids like her, and it would be a good way to get her to attend more church events. Nothing more."

Feigning shock over the phone, Jerome had to laugh at his mother's antics.

"I didn't even say anything! Just that your daddy thinks he hit the jackpot with hiring her and is hoping that she becomes a member of the congregation is all."

"I know you, Mama. You started scheming the second you heard me say her name."

Clearly caught, Evelyn stopped trying to hide her true intentions. "So? I'm your mama! And if a young lady that your daddy already approves of walks into your life, I will not wait for you to do something. I want some more grandbabies to spoil boy!"

Jerome laughed. "See you later this evening. Love you, Mama."

JEROME

Jerome was helping the morning crew with setting up the activity stations for the day when he heard Tasha's voice.

"Morning Rome! Where do you need me?"

Following the sound, he turned to his left and immediately started cheesing at the sight of her. Wearing a pair of old sneakers as he suggested, Tasha looked adorable with her twists pulled up into two separate high buns. The right side she recently had faded a bit and he could see the swirling lines etched onto the side of her temple. Jerome had not seen her in shorts before, which is the only reason that he could think of for staring at her exposed legs and low mid thighs.

"If you tell me that my shorts are too short, be ready to square up, big head," she informed him quickly.

"N-nah, you look great," Jerome croaked out. Hearing some of the guys around him chuckle, he added, "But your shirt, some parents might not approve."

She then looked at her orange top and frowned. "Okay, so it is a little snug, but it was the only top in my closet that had no logos on it! I don't see what—"

Before Tasha could finish her rant, two teenage boys jogged past and collided with one another as they stopped to look at her.

"Yo, eyes up here, jit!" Tasha ordered as the boys slowly looked her in the eye. "Y'all know it's rude to stare, right?" she asked as the two nodded. Tasha then looked around slowly before she leaned in closer toward them and whispered, "Well, it's even more impolite to stare at someone's body parts. One day you might do it to the wrong person and they'll end up curb stomping you into next week."

One boy stepped back as the other one finally spoke to her. "Y-yes ma'am."

Satisfied with his answer, Tasha gave them one more warning as she placed her hands on her hips. "Don't let it happen again, understand?"

When they said nothing, she balled up one of her fists and raised it in the air. "Understand?!"

"Yes ma'am!" they shouted in unison.

"Good. Now gone on somewhere." With the wave of Tasha's hand, the boys sprinted as far away as they could get from her.

Jerome's mouth was slightly opened as Tasha turned back to face him, offering only a casual shrug. "Come with me please so I can find you a volunteer shirt for today."

MID-MORNING QUICKLY became early afternoon, and the small fair was doing well. Jerome had managed to get Tasha into a more appropriate shirt, even after all her protesting. After checking in with each booth, Jerome finally sat down near the admissions booth and took a swig from his bottle of water.

"Hey Jerome!"

He about jumped out of his skin when he felt cold, tiny hands on the back of his neck. "Hi Sister Nina, how are you doing?" he asked, only out of Southern politeness.

"Well, I'm fine now that I get to see you! When will you come back to the midweek classes? We've sure missed seeing you there."

There was no mistaking the way her eyes traveled up and down his frame, and Jerome wanted to put some more distance between them when he saw it.

"Well, I am pretty busy ministering for the younger members these days," he explained.

"But I'm sure Brother Rob is doing a great job in your classes, right?"

She frowned at hearing his reply. "Brother Rob is okay, but you . . . would be a much better *fit*, don't you think?" she purred.

Nina's eyes took in his physique one more time before Jerome spotted Evelyn. Side-stepping the woman to end their conversation, he called out to his mother immediately once he was out of Nina's grasp.

The older woman turned around and her eyes widened as Jerome took her by the hand and led her away in the opposite direction. "Baby, why is you rushing? Your daddy and I just got here," she told him.

Once he was a safe distance away, he bent down to kiss his mother's cheek. "Thank you for coming when you did, Mama. Sister Nina had found me and—"

He didn't get to finish his sentence before Evelyn's scowl was in full effect. "That woman just don't know when to quit! Twice divorced and still out here ready to sin. Just shameful!" Jerome laughed as he looked at the scowl on her face. "It ain't funny, boy. That woman is only a few years younger than me, and here she is, practically throwing it at you every chance she gets!"

Jerome's eyes widened at hearing the more than suggestive slang come from her mouth. "Mama! Where did you hear that kind of talk?" He asked, clearly surprised.

The older woman rolled her eyes at him. "You know, I spend time out in the real world, and I hear things just like you do. Just don't tell ya daddy."

Jerome chuckled as he leaned down to kiss her cheek again. "Yes ma'am."

"Now, where is this Ms. Daye that everyone is talking about these days? I want to meet her."

Of course you do, Mama. You never been one for wasting time. He smiled before taking the staff schedule out of his back pocket and scanning the area to see where she was scheduled to be. "I'll introduce you to her now."

After saying hello to several other church members, Jerome and Evelyn were in front of the kids' painting booth. As they got closer, the two saw Tasha sitting next to three little girls, and one of them was crying. The girls couldn't have been more than eight or nine years old. As Jerome was about to step in, Evelyn grabbed ahold of his shoulder, getting his attention.

"Ms. Tasha! I wanted the rainbow cloud first!" the crying child shouted.

Tasha pulled a few tissues out of a small box and handed them to the younger girl. "I know, and I will paint you a beautiful rainbow cloud soon, okay?"

"But it's not fair! Why they copy me?!" she wailed.

"We ain't copy you Liz, dang!"

"You such a baby!" the other girls said.

Jerome watched as Tasha brought her index finger to her lips before she spoke again to the girls. "There is no need to be upset. Or to shout. Or to name call." She gave each girl a stern look as she stressed each word. "Girls, would you show Liz your clouds please?" she asked gently.

The girls each stuck out their hands and Tasha talked to the little girl again, who now was just sniffling and not crying as loudly as she had been a minute before. "Look at the colors of the other rainbow clouds. What do you see?"

The little girl peeked at her friend's paintings and then back to Tash. "They different colors!"

Tasha nodded as she sent the little girl a soft smile. "We are all different. That's what makes us so special. So when I paint your rainbow cloud, it'll be a little different too."

"Really?"

Tasha grinned as she placed a hand over her heart. "I promise."

The girls looked at their rainbow clouds and smiled.

"Now, what is your favorite color in the whole wide world?"

Jerome and Evelyn watched on as Tasha waited for the young girl to give her an answer.

"Purble!"

Tasha then grabbed her paints and fine brush. "Excellent choice! Why is that your favorite color?" Tasha mixed swirls of colors together on her plastic plate and began lightly drawing with the paint onto her tiny client's hand.

"Cause . . . cause the color purble makes me happy!"

Tasha smiled as she began to softly blow the paint dry. "That's a wonderful answer. All done!"

The girl looked at her hand, admiring the bright purple and gold cloud over a rainbow and gave Tasha a gummy smile as she went running off with her friends.

Jerome, so caught up in watching her, didn't notice Evelyn stepping in front of Tasha.

"Rainbow cloud painting is serious business these days, uh?" she teased.

Tasha grinned before agreeing, "It is, but the payoff is worth it. Would you like a small painting as well, ma'am? Maybe a shooting star or a flaming heart?"

Jerome jogged up to the two women, and before he could say anything, Tasha beat him to it. "Whatever you come to ask about me, big head, can wait. I have a client."

Evelyn laughed, catching Jerome off guard, and Tasha continued, turning her attention to his mother. "You'd think as the man running this event, he'd have something better to do, but he's been policing me all day!" Tasha complained.

"Is that so? This young man troubling you, baby?" Evelyn asked Tasha.

"He means well, I guess. So it's okay." The two ladies shared a laugh, and Jerome finally got a word in.

"Tash, meet my mama, the first lady of Christ's Corner, Mrs. Jerome Grant." If he had his phone out, Jerome would have happily taken a picture of Tasha's face at that moment. She looked like a deer caught in headlights as she slowly glanced between him and Evelyn.

"I-I see the resemblance now." Clearing her throat, Tasha dropped her brush into a cup of fresh water and wiped her hands against her apron.

"It's great to meet you, First Lady. And about what I said earlier—"

"Chile, hush!" Evelyn told Tasha as she brought her into a big hug. Jerome watched as Tasha's eyes widened.

Evelyn stepped back after a minute and looked Tasha over grandly. "So you are the after-school tutor I've heard so much about? When I first suggested that my husband hire someone, I never thought he would bring on a woman. But I am sure glad that he did!"

Tasha lowered her head and started tapping one of her sneakers over the other. "That is kind of you to say ma'am."

Jerome watched as Evelyn gently elbowed Tasha. "Enough of this 'ma'am' nonsense! Call me Evelyn."

"Yes, ma- Is Mrs. Grant okay?" Tasha asked cautiously.

Hearing Tasha's request made Evelyn laugh again. "Alright, I'm sure my husband would love to hear that, as folks usually just call me 'First Lady.' Like I'm married to the president or something."

Tasha smiled. "To them, you're far more important than those sitting in the oval office."

Jerome beamed as he watched their interaction. *Why am I surprised that they are getting along so well?* Before long, Tasha had another happy client, as he and Evelyn left her booth.

Evelyn admired the three shooting stars painted on her left hand.

"So kind and respectful," she mused as they surveyed the fairgrounds. She looked at him and laughed. "She also is one for speaking her mind. Headstrong. I like that."

He liked that quality in Tasha too. Along with so many others, after seeing her with those little ones earlier. The first chance he got, Jerome made sure that he would tell her in person. He was so lost in his thoughts about Tasha, he didn't notice his mother as she looked up at him.

When he finally saw her staring at him, she simply reached out one of her hands and softly touched his cheek.

"It's happening. At last." she said knowingly. Before he could try to protest, she started to walk away. "Go on and get back to work, baby. I'm going to try them briskets from Rock 'em Sock 'em Ribs while there's still some left!"

Now alone, Jerome did as his mother told him to. He took out his schedule again to check in with all the vendors and booths to see that everyone was okay. Looking across the field to see Tasha cleaning up her booth for the next painter, Jerome smiled as he strolled to check on the next station.

"MAN, THIS AIN'T THE business!" Patrick snatched off the worker gloves that made his hands all sweaty and took another break from helping the others clear the carnival for the night. One of the older men looked at Patrick and shook his head.

"You got something to say? Uh?" he sneered, before spitting out of the corner of his mouth. Making himself as comfortable as he could on a nearby bench, Patrick looked around the grounds to see if he could find a girl to introduce to the backseat of his daddy's car for the night. What he saw instead was the food truck trick. She was all smiles with a group of jits, not in puberty yet. *Can't believe her fat ass is out here in those shorts.*

Thinking back to earlier this week, he remembered how she acted towards him at Bottom's Up. *Maybe if I buy something from her little truck, she'll treat me like she should,*

Patrick thought as he went up to The Fast Fix that night. But what he got instead was a stone-faced Tasha who, when she got up to see who was in her service window, served him two middle fingers as she went to sit back down.

"You ain't gonna serve me?!" he shouted before kicking the bottom of her truck. When he did, Patrick noticed a huge black scuff was now on the front of his brand new kicks. Marching inside the club, Patrick went to complain about her to the management, and the new bouncers just laughed at him. That pissed him off, so he went looking for one of the older bouncers. Seeing Rick, a bouncer that he partied with back in the day and bailed out of jail once, Patrick scanned the club and waited for a girl to his liking to come over.

After a few songs, he spotted the high yellow girl that he and Chuck tried to tag-team the night of Wyatt's Bachelor's party. She looked his way and before she could turn her back on him, Patrick grabbed her wrist, making sure she felt his frustration. She winced from his grip as he pulled out a wad of bills and brought them to the front of her face.

"I want to know about that bitch running the truck outside."

"YOU SEE THIS?! WHY is that food truck ho here? And I heard she's working at the church now too!" he spat out as he continued to watch her play with the kids.

"Man, it's been weeks, let it go already," Doug told him.

"Nah man! How she gonna work at a place like that and show her face in the Lord's house?" Patrick took out his phone while watching more people pass by them at the jamboree. He scrolled through his contacts before finding the number he was looking for and putting the phone on speaker.

"Yo! What's good!"

"Aye Marcus! You still got your high school yearbook?" *I think Pastor Grant needs to know who his latest congregation member really is.*

"Yeah, it's at my mama's house though. Why you need it?" Marcus asked.

With his eyes still on Tasha, he saw her wave goodbye to the kids and walk over to the first lady and Jerome.

"You'll find out. Just bring it to the church thing tonight," Patrick told him before ending the call. He went back to pretending to work as he listened to the conversation between Tasha, Jerome, and the first lady of Christ's Corner.

"Again, it was nice to meet you, Mrs. Evelyn," Tasha said.

He rolled his eyes as the first lady gave Tasha a hug. *I bet you won't be so quick to hug on her when you find out where she's heading.*

He continued to watch them as Jerome pulled her to the side and asked, "Do you really have to go now? I was hoping that we could ride on the Ferris wheel together."

Patrick almost laughed out loud. *This dude really feeling this bitch! Oh shiiiiiittt!*

Tasha then took one of Jerome's hands into hers, and Patrick stopped pretending to eavesdrop all together as he looked at the way Tasha returned Jerome's stare.

"I told you I have a group shoot today, and I have to leave by 3pm to set up. I'm sorry."

Oh, so y'all out here catching feelings for one another? I'mma have to end that right quick, Patrick vowed as he watched Tasha leave the field. *When I'm done exposing you bitch, Jerome ain't gonna want nothing to do with your dumpy ass!*

Just as the crew was loading the last of the equipment from the entrance of the fair, Patrick spotted Marcus walking his way with the yearbook. "Took you long enough," Patrick said as Marcus rolled his eyes.

"You lucky I came at all! I still don't know why you need this mess, anyway."

Ignoring Marcus, Patrick snatched the book from his hands and started turning the pages. Finally landing on a picture of Tasha from their junior year of high school, a sick grin slowly spread across his face. "Help me find Pastor Grant," Patrick demanded.

The two walked and saw the older folks standing around listening to the pastor. *Just the man I was looking for!* Patrick thought as he weaved his way to the front. Happy with the size of the crowd at the moment, Patrick listened on as Pastor Grant spoke.

"It's events like this here jamboree that help us keep the church united and keep the young ones out of these streets."

A few of the men nodded as the women shouted in agreement. Patrick wanted to roll his eyes, but he knew someone would see him. Focusing harder on Pastor Grant, he waited until the man stopped speaking before approaching him.

"You right Pastor about this jamboree. Thank you for watching over the flock and putting together this event." Patrick easily inflated the man's ego as he prepared to cause a scene.

"Of course, young man! As the leader of Christ's Corner, it is my honor to do all I can for my congregation," Pastor Grant boomed.

"That is why I wanted to see you tonight, sir. I have recently learned that we have a new member in our church. Someone that is now tutoring the kids?" Patrick slowly inquired.

He watched as the older man's face lit up, and he wanted to knock out his dentures. *Why is everyone so hung up on this bitch?*

"Well, Ms. Daye is not an official member of Christ's Corner yet, but that hopefully will change," the pastor informed Patrick.

Let me squash this mess now, he thought as he opened the yearbook again and handed it to Pastor Grant. "I really think you should reconsider that, Pastor. Is this girl here the new tutor?"

Patrick watched on as the Pastor looked at the photo and nodded.

"So, you hired someone that works at a *gentlemen's club* to tutor our youth, Pastor?" Patrick asked loud enough for a few of the older men to hear. They all stopped walking and stared, just as he expected.

The Pastor narrowed his eyes at Patrick before he asked him with a growl, "What did you just say to me, boy?"

Patrick took out his phone and showed the man a picture that he took of Tasha at The Fast Fix when he left the club last night. The man squinted before recognition settled in his eyes. Patrick took that as his cue to command the crowd.

"That is the same person, right, Pastor? The tutor you hired for the church? Working at a gentlemen's club? And I hear that her mama can be seen on any given Sunday, battling her demons with a group of other loose women and street dealers inside the condemned houses on Marley Court Avenue."

The pastor's eyes widened before he looked out into the crowd of slacked-jawed members of his church. Pastor Grant tried in vain to say something, anything, to rid himself of what Patrick had shared, but Patrick cut him off to talk to the growing crowd.

"How many of your children have been to the church to be tutored by this loose woman? Why is something like this allowed in our fine congregation?"

One woman stepped forward and pointed at the pastor. "My child is already fighting demons! Skipping school and getting into fights. Pastor Grant, how could you allow such a woman to be Patricia's tutor?" the woman shrieked.

Pastor Grant backed away with his hands raised. "I-I had no idea about any of this!" the old man stammered out.

As more of the crowd yelled their shock and disgust, Patrick tried not to grin. *My work here is done. If I hurry and leave this mess, I can make it to BU as soon as they open for happy hour.* Patrick turned to leave when he heard the golden preacher kid arrive.

"What is all this? What are y'all saying about Ms. Daye?" he questioned the crowd as they all grew silent from his presence.

Pastor Grant marched up to his son, face twisted in frustration and not enough embarrassment for Patrick's liking as he barked, "Did you know about this boy? This girl working at a gentlemen's club?"

A beat passed before Jerome answered. "She works at the food truck outside the club, not inside the club," he told the crowd evenly.

Patrick turned back around, intrigued by this new side of Jerome. "So, you knew! And said nothing!" someone in the crowd shouted. "What about her mama? You know that kind of loose woman runs in the family!"

The pastor tapped his finger into Jerome's chest. "You let that loose woman teach across from your office for weeks! Knowing this information?!"

Jerome frowned as he looked down at his daddy, and Patrick enjoyed seeing the exchange. *Looks like our PK just needed a taste of honey to find his backbone.*

"That is the last phrase I would use to describe Tasha Daye. She works hard and loves tutoring the kids at Christ's Corner," Jerome stated proudly.

Two women from the crowd wasted no time in speaking after that with cutting remarks. "I bet she is hard working . . . with knee pads on."

"Just like her mama. Anything for the pipe."

The men around them chuckled as Pastor Grant hung his head, but Jerome stood firm as he scolded the women, "You call yourself a woman of God, yet you speak that way about another sister?"

Patrick watched in awe as Jerome continued, not waiting for a response, "Tasha is kind, patient, and great at tutoring. Her work outside of the church is not ideal, but it is also not illegal. And what her mama is or isn't doing is not Tasha's burden to carry. So why should it matter to all of you?"

Patrick's lips turned down as he saw his crowd slowly begin to agree with Jerome. Thankfully, his boy Mitch spoke up from in the back of the group.

"So you okay with your girlfriend working there. That don't mean we have to be okay with it!"

Patrick grinned as he spoke over Jerome. "Yeah! The folks here have a right to say that they don't want that kind of woman tutoring their kids!"

Seeing the crowd return to his side again, Patrick asked the pastor loudly, "If she continues to work there and does not repent, then why should this woman be allowed to tutor the kids, Pastor?" The crowd clapped and nodded as Patrick added. "If she won't do that much, shouldn't we find another tutor who has a more . . . decent job?"

Pastor Grant looked at Patrick before holding out his hands to silence the crowd. "I have heard you all, and I agree. If Ms. Daye doesn't repent and stop working at that establishment, I will be forced to find a new tutor."

Jerome looked like he wanted to swing on his daddy and Patrick loved seeing it. *Looks like you gonna lose your not-so- little girlfriend now, punk ass PK.*

Tasha

Being inside the club was still foreign to her, but after all the girls arrived and she got her lighting set up for the shoot, Tasha soon felt right at home. Since she knew most of the girls beforehand, getting them to take her advice on poses now and then as she worked the room for their mini sessions went much smoother than she initially thought it would. Occasionally, a girl would ask to see her photo, and Tasha was happy to show off her work.

"Damn Tash, you really know what you doing with that thing," Trixie said as she looked at a few of her shots toward the end of the shoot.

"I know a little something something," Tasha replied, feeling her cheeks warm up from the compliment. "By the way, thanks for messaging me for this gig. Remind me to give you a discount too on your digital orders once I have them ready for you to preview."

Trixie grinned as she snapped her fingers in a figure eight shape around Tasha. "Hell yeah! Good looking out!"

Breaking down her equipment before the club opened for the evening, Tasha felt like she was walking on a cloud as she went to her car to leave. The feeling she got after an amazing photoshoot was the best rush ever, and she couldn't wait to get back to the house to edit her work.

Tasha was so caught up in the afterglow, she didn't notice Patrick as he walked over and leaned against the passenger side of her ride. When she carefully put all her things in the backseat and saw his figure in the window, Tasha rolled her eyes as she closed her door.

"Aren't you full of *tricks*?" he taunted. "Working out in that hot ass truck, at the church, and now you taking pictures of the girls? Where do you find the time?" Patrick asked as he made his way over to the driver's side of her car.

Not in the mood for his foolishness, Tasha reached into her back pocket and swiftly unlocked her stun gun. Once he was within a few feet, she directed it at his face and smiled as his eyes widened. "My best trick is making assholes like you piss themselves from the voltage on my stunner."

Patrick took another step toward her, and Tasha pressed gently on the stun gun, letting him see the hot blue currents of electricity for himself. Quickly, he backed away several feet, giving Tasha enough distance that she felt comfortable enough to climb into the driver's side of her car. Keeping her windows rolled up, Tasha gave him a one-finger salute as she reversed her ride and drove away.

JEROME'S SILENCE DURING their breakfast should have been her first clue that something was up. He would normally ask Tasha questions about the weekend and want to see what photos she had taken. Instead, Jerome was almost mute that morning as he stared at her while playing with his cheese grits, sausage, and eggs.

"You okay, Rome? All morning you been awfully quiet," she finally asked as he came back into the office from washing their trays in the kitchen. From the look on his face, you would've thought that someone kicked his favorite dog.

"I'm good Tash, just worried about . . . nevermind."

She looked at him from across his desk and quietly sighed. Tasha didn't know what was going on, but she knew that she couldn't stand to see the torn look on his face. Quickly, she stood up and walked over to his side of the office desk before sitting on the edge. Holding out a fist, Tasha brought it up to meet his eye and a half grin finally showed up on his face as he tapped his fist against hers. "Whatever it is, I promise, it's not nearly as bad as the sour look on your face." she told him gently.

Jerome looked up at her and Tasha felt queasy as she held his stare. Feeling the need to breathe and stretch her arms, Tasha put some distance between them and made her way back to her office.

At 2:13 pm, Tasha left Patricia a message asking if she would be coming in for their session today. As she went over her notes on the students for the day, Tasha heard the church doors open and stood to greet her student. When Pastor Grant walked into her office, she was a little thrown off but worked on keeping it professional. She waved at the older man, and he remained in the doorway.

"Patricia's mama removed her from your tutoring sessions."

Tasha frowned. "May I ask why?"

The older man stared at her and shook his head. "It has come to the attention of our congregation that your other place of employment is not becoming of someone associated with Christ's Corner."

As he spoke, Tasha thought back to Jerome's behavior earlier and connecting the dots became much clearer. *He knew this would happen today*, she realized. Knowing that made her feel almost as sad as Jerome looked this morning.

"What does what I do outside of my tutoring here have to do with anything?" Tasha asked sharply.

The pastor narrowed his eyes at her before scoffing, "Well, Ms. Daye, you cannot seriously think that it is okay to work at such a place and still be employed by this church."

Tasha laughed, "Let me make sure I understand you correctly. I'm being asked to choose between my primary source of income, or to continue working for almost less than minimum wage at this job? For the sake of *your* church's image?"

Several seconds passed, but it was enough time to allow Tasha to grab her belongings and walk to the office's entrance. As she now stood in front of Pastor Grant, the older man cleared his throat and looked up at her as he nervously wheezed out, "In that case, I will consider today as the beginning of your two-week notice."

"You can consider that if you like, but I don't do notices." Tasha didn't look back as she walked to the main entrance and hopped into her car.

Great, just great. What am I going to do now? Tasha thought furiously as she parked her car and jogged up the stairs to the apartment.

Quickly letting herself in, she kicked her flats into a corner and flopped down on the couch. Her last few photography sessions had paid well enough, so she made sure to pay rent in advance. Taking out her laptop, Tasha turned it on and waited for the sign-in screen to show up before logging in. After a trip to the kitchen, Tasha was fully armed with a big spoon and a pint of ice cream. She looked over her finance chart to see how much time she had to find more work. Digging into the creamy sweetness of her pecan ice cream, Tasha did the math and was not impressed.

According to her calculations, she'd be brokety-broke in ninety days if she couldn't find another gig. But after dealing with Christ's Corner, Tasha wondered if she even wanted to work for someone else. Her hours at The Fast Fix were good, and she had to admit that she'd rather braid water than go back to being on her feet all day with a retail job. To distract herself for a few more hours, Tasha finished up editing the girls' photos from last weekend. As she sent out the preview links by email, an ad for a photography internship caught her eye, and Tasha mindlessly clicked on the advertisement link.

Have you always wanted to travel, but thought the means were out of your reach?

If you have a DSLR, then let The Rebel Shots in Argentina make your dream a reality!

Their delivery line was a little lame, but Tasha had time. Checking out the website as she polished off the pint of ice cream, it at least seemed legit. And she had wanted to get a passport to travel since high school, but something always stopped her from making it happen. The company had a simple enough application process, so Tasha filled out everything. Worst case scenario, she would never hear from them. But as she was choosing which photos to submit for the application, Tasha decided. *It's time for me to become legit in the photography business.*

As the ball of excitement grew in her stomach, Tasha thought back on what happened today and wasn't even a little mad. Having to choose between Bottom's Up and Christ's Corner was just the push she needed to finally make her skills with a camera more than just a side hustle. Remembering her words of encouragement to Jerome before seeing Pastor Grant that morning, Tasha broke out into a giggle as she picked up her phone to send him a quick text message.

Wanna see if we can get to the next level tonight on that game you bought?
-Tash

"ONE DAY YOU GONNA GET us kicked out of BU for real, with your dumbass!" Doug shouted at Patrick as he lit a cigarette.

Doug and Jamal had left BU just before closing time and finally caught up with Patrick after he drove to the local park. Earlier that night, he was told twice to not touch the girls, and with none of his old security guards on duty, it didn't take long for two new, eager bouncers to hoist Patrick up against the wall next to the main stage. It had been a while since they'd gotten to make an example out of a handsy customer, so they took turns bouncing him around like a hockey puck as they led him outside.

Jamal laughed as Doug re-enacted the scene, and Patrick wanted to put his cigarette out inside his friend's eye.

It's that food truck bitch's fault! I swear I can't stand her ass!
"Whatever! Why y'all ain't come out with me anyway?" Patrick
questioned, making the guys laugh even harder.

"Why would I volunteer to leave my dance—that I paid for—to be
outside with you, bruh?! That's just stupid on stupid," Jamal told him as
he kept walking.

Before Patrick could say another word, he bumped into Jamal as
Doug backed into him.

"What the he—" Jamal started to say before Doug put his hand
over his mouth.

"Look at this shit right here!" Doug whispered as he pointed across
the street.

Patrick and Jamal did as he instructed and both of their mouths
hung open as they watched Tasha standing in front of Jerome's opened
apartment door.

"Well, shit!" Doug breathed out.

"I thought Marcus was lying at the fair about these two being
together!" Jamal added.

Patrick took out his phone, and the others did the same to take
pictures of Jerome and Tasha. There was just enough light from the
street lamppost to see Jerome walk Tasha to her car. The two were
clearly hyped about something, as they were all smiles when Tasha
opened her car door. Before she got in the car, Jerome held the door for
her and leaned in to say something close to her ear. Whatever he said
made Tasha cover her mouth to stop from laughing out loud.

"Dammmmn! They really go together, y'all!" Jamal said as he took
another picture.

Doug looked over Jamal's shoulder before thinking out loud, "I
always wondered what his type was . . . No wonder he never dated
anyone at church."

Jamal looked behind him and asked his friend, "Why you
wondering about what his type is? Bruh, you sound gay!"

The two went on bickering as Patrick continued to watch Jerome and Tasha. *She almost lit me up tonight, and now this ho letting PK push all up on her?!*

Tasha finally got into her ride and drove away. They watched Jerome as he looked on at Tasha leaving.

"Look at his face, y'all! That thick pudding must've been sweet!" Jamal shouted.

As Jerome turned around to go back inside his apartment, Patrick fumed even harder thinking about the look on Tasha's face earlier at BU. He knew for sure that she would have used that stunner on him, and seeing her being all sweet with Jerome just now pissed him off.

Remembering that Pastor Grant recently started to send out a newsletter to the congregation, his way of connecting with them outside of church, Patrick went to one of the most recent messages. Seeing that the email had been sent to over a hundred people from the church, he then attached all the pictures that he had just taken of Jerome and Tasha. Once they were all uploaded, Patrick pressed 'send' before getting in his car to go back across town to go home for the night.

JEROME

After hearing the exchange between Senior and Tasha that morning, Jerome quietly slipped out of the church using the backdoor exits. He was not in the mood to listen to anything that Senior had to say that day, so he sent out emails letting the parents know that youth bible study would be canceled.

Finding himself with no place to go, Jerome went home to see his mother. Letting himself in with his spare key, Jerome called out to her but didn't hear an answer. Not wanting Senior to know that he'd been there when he was supposed to be at church, Jerome sent Evelyn a text asking her if she was busy. Minutes went by without an answer, so he left.

As he drove around aimlessly, it became clear to Jerome that he really had no social life. No wonder when he told folks about his plans to become a rapper they would laugh at him. He never spent any time anywhere but at the church or at home. That was something he wanted to change, but really didn't know how. Instead of going home to sulk, he parked his car at a nearby plaza to get out and walk along the sidewalk. Taking in the other strangers going about their day, he enjoyed the feeling of the sun on his skin as he sat down on a bench and took out his phone to write.

Instead of writing verses like he intended, Jerome found himself thanking God for the day—how brilliant the sun shone and renewed his spirit, how he was thankful that he had another day to share the joy in his heart with those who were dearest to him. When Jerome read the lines again, Tasha's face appeared.

The memories of how they met and became friends over these last few months flashed in front of him, and Jerome went on typing about how having her in his life made him feel. Reading the last lines he wrote, Jerome smiled as he titled the note 'Heavenly Gifts' and sent it to his email address. As he stood up and stretched, a few members of the church saw him, and Jerome waved as he went back to his car to head home. Before he put the key in the ignition, his phone vibrated. Thinking it was his mother, Jerome took it out to see what her reply was from earlier. He broke out into laughter as he read the message from Tasha instead. Sending her back a simple okay as he revved the engine, Jerome decided to order a pizza as he made his way back home to clean up while waiting for Tasha to arrive at his place later.

THE TWO FELL INTO THEIR new routine like old dominos as Tasha made it to his apartment later that night. Jerome already had the game set up and was waiting for Tasha to bring over their drinks as she sat down on the floor next to him and grabbed a slice of pizza.

"Why are you still driving with your controller, big head?" she joked as Jerome made his player run up the pyramid and jump down quickly to touch the flag at the end of the quest.

"Why do you care what I do? It's my scene to beat. Let me play in peace," he told Tasha as she laughed.

"I can't help it! Tina used to drive the controller back when we played this game, and it drove me nuts!" she explained as she kept laughing. "You look weird! Just stop already!" Tasha said as Jerome exaggerated the movement even more while moving on to the next level.

After a few hours, they finally managed to level up within the game, but they were almost too tired to celebrate.

"So this is what I missed out on? Spending hours staring at a TV screen and sitting in the same spot to play with a computer?" Jerome asked jokingly.

Tasha scrunched up her face at him before nodding, "Yes!"

Sunday services were tomorrow, and Jerome wasn't surprised when Tasha said it was time for her to leave. She never spent the night on Saturdays, saying that even the Lord had a day of rest and she needed one too. Turning the game off, Jerome walked Tasha out to her car and reminded her to text him once she got home. Before she hopped into her car, he held her driver's side door as he leaned down and whispered in her ear, "If you don't text me, I'll drive all night with my controller to find you like I did earlier."

Tasha snorted and shook her head, "You are really something else, you know that Rome?"

Jerome's heart still soared hearing her use the nickname, and he stared out into the night as her car left the parking lot.

MORNING CAME SOONER than Jerome wanted it to, and he stretched deeply into his bed before getting up and going to the bathroom to shower. Wrapping a towel around his waist after stepping out of the shower and walking into his room again, Jerome looked around and sighed. He tried to think of why everyone would be so against Tasha. He even prayed that God would show him what he couldn't see because of the new feelings in his heart for her, but nothing came.

Once inside the church, he entered the security code to disarm the church's alarm system and walked to his office. On the way, he passed Tasha's office. Jerome took a second to picture her inside, going over her notes and listening to the local jazz radio station. At first the endless instrumental sounds used to get on his nerves, but now Jerome knew he would miss hearing it in between her lessons. The sounds from Tasha's office that let him know she was still there and the quiet now would just be a painful reminder that she was gone.

Church went well enough, but Jerome couldn't shake the feeling that everyone was staring at him as he sat in the first pew next to Evelyn. It didn't bother him; growing up in the church, Jerome was used to folks staring at him. But something about their stares today made him uneasy. Senior hadn't said a word to him, and Jerome was fine with that too, though as the sermon went on, he felt like Senior was silently praying over him with each word he shouted into the microphone. Once the service ended, he helped his mother up from the pew. She didn't need his help, but he loved spending time with her and getting her to smile.

"How you doing, baby? I heard about Tasha."

Jerome knew she would ask eventually and was thankful that she waited until after church service. Sighing, he looked down at her and answered her honestly, "I'm fine Mama, but I just don't see why everyone is so against Tasha. What was her sin?" Feeling his mother take one of his hands into her own, Jerome closed his eyes briefly before they walked out into the hall to join the others that stayed for juice and cookies in the church's kitchen.

"You know how these folks are, baby. Anyone new to the flock is judged heavily. It's how they try to protect the congregation," she reminded him gently before joining the other sisters to help pass out cookies and drinks.

Jerome nodded before standing in line with the others. Hearing laughter behind him, Jerome turned toward the sound and caught a glimpse of one member looking down at his phone. Before he could say hello, the man and his friend both put their phones away and stared straight ahead in line.

"Jerome Earl Grant Junior! Come here NOW!"

Jerome knew all eyes were on him after hearing Senior call him just now.

Still frustrated with the way his father let Tasha go the other day, Jerome took his time walking toward him. Jerome watched as his father tried to show him something on his phone before giving up and snatching another church member's phone from their hands and thrusting the screen into his face. Seeing a picture of him saying goodnight to Tasha, Jerome took longer than he meant to to look back at his father as he stared down at Tasha's face.

"Is this why you have been acting strange and defending her actions? Just what were you two doing at this time of night together?!" his father demanded.

Afraid of saying anything that would make the situation worse, Jerome kept his eyes on Senior as he waited for him to finish talking.

"You may not care about what I think, but remember, the Lord sees everything and will judge us when the time comes."

Jerome waited for his father to hand the phone back to its owner before speaking. "Then I have nothing to fear. The most high knows what is in my heart, and I have done nothing wrong."

Jerome saw Evelyn pushing members aside to get to him, not bothering to look at anyone as they tried to show her what they were all looking at on their phones. "Baby, what is going on?" she asked him once she was in between Jerome and his father.

"I bet that's what they were calling each other in this pic," someone whispered, getting a few others around them to burst out into laughter.

Jerome could feel his blood pressure rising and had to focus on his mother to keep cool. "Ma'am, someone took pictures of a friend leaving my apartment last night and sent them out to everyone in the church," he answered evenly.

Senior shoo'd Evelyn to stand behind him, and that made Jerome's eye twitch as his father began questioning him again. "You ain't the least bit ashamed? To be out with that woman at that hour?"

Jerome stared down at his father. "Why would I be? She is my friend and we are not doing anything wrong." Before his father spoke again, Jerome continued, "The person walking around late at night to take and send pictures with ill intent should be ashamed of themselves."

The group of members with their phones out quickly begin tapping on their screens. A few immediately put their phones away afterwards, but the member closest to Jerome kept his phone out and looked up at him as he handed Jerome the phone. Taking the phone, Jerome went to the sender's information and rolled his head in disbelief.

"Was Patrick here for today's services?" Looking around the kitchen, Jerome didn't see Patrick, but he found Jamal and Marcus trying to reach the backdoor entrance. The group followed his gaze, and the two men froze as they realized everyone was now watching them. Leaving his father's side, Jerome marched over to them and looked at them both.

"Were you with Patrick when he took those pictures?" Jerome asked.

Jamal looked around as Marcus scoffed in Jerome's face, "Why is that any of your business? It ain't our fault that your down-low relationship was exposed."

Completely done with the whispers and allegations about him and Tasha, Jerome's entire face changed as Marcus and Jamal stepped back against the wall behind them. His hands itched, and he quickly brought them out in front of the two of them. "There is no 'down low' relationship to expose! And I want answers!" Jerome suddenly laughed at the ridiculousness of it all before rounding on the group behind him.

"All y'all are bothered by Tasha, and I want to know why? Besides a few pictures, do any of you know anything about her? If you did, then you wouldn't dare be out here creating gossip about her the way you are today. It's shameful! And she's done nothing to warrant it from any of y'all!" Frustrated with everyone around him, Jerome looked at his mother apologetically as he pushed open the back door to leave.

THE KITCHEN WAS FULL of chatter once Jerome left, and Senior was not happy. As Jamal and Marcus tried to make their way to join the others, the pastor stopped them.

"Come to my office. Now."

Senior waited for the two to show up to his office and shut the door as he looked the two of them straight in the eye. "Were you two with Patrick when he took those pictures? Remember where you are before answering that question." He watched as one of the young men nodded.

"Good." Seeing the shocked expressions on their faces, Senior continued, "This Daye girl has completely beguiled my boy, but with your help, we are going to fix that."

They heard a knock at the door.

"Come in!"

A tall, husky man entered the room. He walked up to Senior and showed him a set of keys. Standing in front of the men in his office, Senior spoke again, "That boy of mine was coddled too much by his mama, and it's my fault for not stepping in earlier like I should have, but today that is good news for us. Before he moved out, he gave his mama a spare key to his new place, and I had Eugene here secure it secretly after seeing those pictures today." He patted the larger man on the back. "I know it is a sin to steal, but since we are returning this key to my wife, it won't count."

Jamal, confused and ready to leave, asked, "Why are we here, Pastor?"

The older man leaned down to look him in the eye. "You two are going to help Eugene here get inside my boy's apartment so he can put some cameras up that will finally show us just how this Ms. Daye is luring my boy away from the righteous path."

Chapter Six
Deliverance

Tasha

T "I still can't believe that I'm giving up my warm and fluffy bed for you," Tasha said as she helped Jerome unfold the oversized blanket before sitting down to enjoy the view.

That Sunday afternoon, Jerome called Tasha to ask if she wanted to get away from town with him. At first she thought he was joking, but as she listened to him more on the line, Tasha could hear the urgency in his voice. Strangely, Tasha felt completely okay with being out of town with Jerome. And remembering how he was there for her after what went down with her sisters months ago, Tasha felt the need to be there for him now.

As soon as she said yes, Jerome asked her to think of a place that she'd like to visit, and not even an hour later he was knocking on her door.

Alexa and Rachel could barely keep their shock and squeals to themselves as Jerome arrived at the house. He said hello to them and waited for Tasha to grab her bag so they could take off. The two drove quietly as Tasha entered the location's address into his GPS and soon found herself trying to stay awake.

Stopping once to refill the tank, Tasha could see that the distance away from home was already improving Jerome's mood. Bejon Beach was empty by the time they arrived after having dinner at the nearest diner, and that suited Tasha just fine. She wasn't ready to admit it out loud yet, but Tasha loved having Jerome all to herself. Tasha sighed happily as they sat and listened to the small waves meet the shore.

"I'm so glad Alexa let me have a day vacay from The Fast Fix for this."

"Me too," Jerome agreed.

"And to still get paid too? Really helps keep down my living expenses for the month." From the corner of her eye, Tasha saw Jerome's jaw tighten. "It's okay," she whispered gently.

"No, it ain't. He had no right —" Jerome started, but Tasha interrupted his thoughts as she placed a hand on top of his.

"But it's done, Rome. I always make a way," she assured him. Tasha could see him struggle with what to say next, so she gently squeezed on his hand to get his attention. As he looked up at her, Tasha winked at him, and Jerome's gaze softened.

"Why do you keep calling me that?" he finally asked.

"I want to make sure that you know you two are different. Is it working?"

"Yeah."

"Good. Now tell me about your day before the sun sets."

Tasha half listened to Jerome filling her in on how he was passing his time between finishing his album and volunteering more at the hard-of-hearing center he found a few weeks ago while he was out with his mama.

"It's been nice to meet and get to know others with a deaf or hard-of-hearing family member. They get to see their loved ones more than I see Eva though. I want to change that someday."

Tasha spent more time staring at his facial features, noting his thick brows, the glint in his warm brown eyes, and how the change from late day to early evening casted his deep skin into smooth gradients of brown to a faint, muted hue that reminded her of an angel oak tree.

"I wish it was Senior that left instead of Eva all those years ago . . ."

Tasha looked into his eyes then and didn't like what she saw as Jerome stared out at the waves. Before the sun went down for the day, she wanted to help him be at peace somehow.

"I know you're still angry at how that all went down with your folks and Eva. Having Senior fire me from Christ's Corner probably didn't help you on your way toward forgiving him. And right now, that anger feels good. But Rome, don't let pride get in the way of making peace while you still can. I spent years doing what you're doing with Senior right now with my family. Do you need a reminder of how that all went down?"

He leveled his eyes onto hers and groaned, "But he's the one always in the wrong. Why should I have to be the one to make amends?"

Tasha smiled softly as she said, "I'm not the bible reader between us, but I'm sure there's something in that book that will tell you the answer to that."

Jerome slowly shook his head. "You right. Mama's been quoting scriptures to me about this since last week, but dang Tash! Why I got to be the bigger person in all this mess?"

Seeing him hang his head and then quickly looking up and over her shoulder, Tasha was struck with an idea of how to soothe his worries. At least for a while. "Can I shoot a few shots of you?"

Jerome chuckled dryly. "I thought we were working on my problems, but you wanna take pictures instead?"

Tasha shook her head. "Taking pictures of you ain't work. And it ain't even really for me. You'll see what I mean."

"Why should I agree to this?"

Rolling her eyes, Tasha quickly explained, "The sun is about to set, and I want to give you these images as a reminder."

Jerome lifted one of his eyebrows at her and smirked. "A reminder of what?"

"That no matter what challenges come your way, you'll see them through to see a brighter day. And in the end, hopefully you will also become a better person for it." She could see him press his lips together, as if he wanted to say something more, so Tasha leaned her shoulders against his. "You got more on your mind?"

This time, when he looked her way, Tasha noticed in almost slow motion as Jerome's eyes softened. And it was more of a captivating view than the one in front of them in that moment, causing her to take in shallow breaths as she waited for him to say more.

"How can you still find so much joy in life? You always find the brightness in everyone. How do you do that?"

Blinking, Tasha managed to refocus and think of a way to answer his question. One that would change the subject, because she didn't trust her emotions if she were to tell him the full truth to what he just asked her. Remembering what she'd asked Jerome before, Tasha smiled at him and picked up her bag. "I don't see the brightness in everyone, just those that can't let bad times steal their shine. That's all you, preacher's kid."

She immediately saw his lips press together, and before Jerome could try to ask her again, Tasha spoke, "So can I take your picture now, or..."

Jerome stared at Tasha for a beat before rolling his eyes. "You ain't even got a camera with you, Tash."

She almost breathed a sigh of relief as Jerome let her change the subject. Grinning wildly, Tasha scrambled to open up her messenger bag and retrieved a small DSLR camera.

"Oh really? Then what is this?" Tasha sang out as she waved her camera in his face. Hearing Jerome's laughter above the waves as she set the aperture and ISO that was needed to capture the moment, Tasha held her camera up to her face as she began calling out small suggestions to Jerome on where to direct his eyes so she could make use of the sunlight left in the surrounding background.

"Look over my right shoulder again please," she instructed. Holding out her left hand, Tasha pointed her index finger into the sky and slowly twirled it around. "Follow my finger please . . . with those patient eyes of yours. Great!"

Jerome soon turned his eyes back to her.

"You think my eyes are patient looking?"

Snapping one last photo, Tasha answered him honestly, "Yeah. And forgiving as well, so I know you'll do what's right in the end."

As she went to put her camera away, Jerome's hand was on hers. "Wait. I wanna take some pictures of you too."

Not prepared for that request, Tasha stuttered out. "Wh-what?"

"Better yet, let's take a picture together!" Jerome grinned.

A wave of uneasiness came over Tasha, and she felt as though she was being asked to walk naked in the street. "Are you sure? What if some—"

Snatching the camera away from Tasha and holding it up midair, Jerome's voice was free and light as he continued, "C'mon! Bring it in so I can take the photo already."

Tasha narrowed her eyes at him as she leaned in closer to him. "Do you even know how to use that?" she joked.

Not bothering to answer her, Jerome pressed down on the front button and quickly whipped the camera around to see the picture he took. Smugly, he showed it to Tasha. "How's that?"

The sun had created a nearly perfect backlight for them in the shot. At that moment, seeing Jerome's blinding smile as Tasha grinned while looking up at him, she knew she was falling for him. She decided to put those feelings away to examine at another time.

"Beginner's luck! Let's see you do it again, big head."

Jerome smiled down at her again and accepted her challenge with a few new terms of his own. "Okay! But if you really like the next . . . five or six shots, you have to agree to come to Christ's Corner next week."

Tasha tried to grab her camera back from Jerome, but he held it just out of reach as he continued. "And if you don't like any of them, then..."

There was nothing Jerome could say to make Tasha accept this bet, but she enjoyed seeing this more relaxed and playful side of him.

"Then I will work at The Fast Fix for you. For three nights straight." Except that.

Tasha stared at him as she blinked incredulously at his terms. "Are you serious right now?"

"Yeah! But you have to be honest. Remember, you can lie to me, but you can't lie to the Lord," he told her sternly.

Jerome looked too pleased with himself for Tasha not to accept his terms, so she simply nodded as he turned the camera back on from sleep mode and started clicking away.

JEROME

He knew Tasha only agreed to be here because of the deal they made the week before, but seeing her sitting in the back pew made him nervous. She showed up wearing all black, with her twists, normally flowing in and around her face, tucked away in easily the tightest low bun he'd ever seen.

She even managed to swoop a few over her mini side fade, he noted sadly.

Did being here really make her that uncomfortable? The pianist began the morning welcome song, and Jerome had to pull his attention away from Tasha. His mother sat in her normal seat in the front row, though today she was not wearing one of her matching dress and hat combos. If Jerome didn't know better, he'd think that Evelyn had dressed Tasha, as both women were dressed in a similar style. Though his mother still showcased her face with the usual makeup and pearls.

He thought back to when he was a little boy and he used to watch her get ready for service in front of her ivory vanity mirror. One day, he finally got the courage to ask her why she put all that stuff on her face. Instead of being upset with him, his mother laughed.

"I know the Lord knows what's in my heart. Doesn't mean I can't show the world what's in there too with a little help now and then."

His daddy walked in at that moment and smiled grandly. "The perfect wife, that is your mama! Always looking her best for service, being a model beacon of obedience for the other women in our congregation."

Jerome could still remember seeing his mother's face after Senior spoke and leaned down to kiss her cheek. It was brief, but the smile she showed Jerome before his father spoke looked much different from the one the two had shared moments before he arrived. It was as if a cloud had rolled in front of the sun. Still bright, but with a warning of an overcast or rain.

He heard the pianist end the song, and before Senior spoke at the pit, he looked out at Evelyn again. Her head was turned towards the back of the church where Tasha was seated. Too interested in this new development, Jerome kept his eyes on the two women as Senior began his service.

Tasha locked eyes with Evelyn, and the two smiled at one another. Evelyn gently raised her hand and gestured for Tasha to come sit next to her, but Tasha quickly shook her hand. He saw Evelyn then tilt her head and place a hand to the side of her face before patting the temple of her head. Tasha must've been confused at first, as she squinted her eyes at her. Then Jerome saw Evelyn do something he had never seen her do in church. She openly grinned as she reached up and unclipped her hair pin, letting her bangs fall forward.

He wasn't the only one shocked by this, as Tasha's eyes widened. Now understanding what she saw earlier, Tasha raised her hands behind her head and released her twists from their bun.

Jerome saw her close her eyes as she then ran her fingers through the front of her hair and almost gasped as he saw the recent work of her mini side fade. Two musical staffs were etched into the fade with a treble clef on one end and a bass clef on the other. Both he and his mother smiled at the sight.

My God, she is beautiful.

After that, Evelyn turned her attention back to her husband. But as she nodded in agreement with Senior's words, Evelyn looked at Jerome from the pews and winked. Blinking a few times, Jerome willed himself to not think about what just happened. He would ask his mother about all that later. Soon it was his turn to take to the pit and announce the weekly church announcements before the deacons began preparing for the tithes offering.

"Th-thank you all for supporting and worshipping with us here at Ch-Christ's Corner. I hope to see you after the service to discuss taking part in getting more of our young members a chance to do some good in the community in Christ's name. Head Deacon, please begin the offerings."

His eyes were on Tasha the entire time he spoke. Jerome hadn't stuttered that much since first speaking in the pit. He knew Senior would be speaking to him soon. Taking his seat again as the head deacon began leading the offerings, Jerome avoided making eye contact with him. Instead, he looked out into the pews and found his gaze back on Tasha. Before the deacon assigned to her pew could walk to her, Jerome felt uneasy. *Why he gotta look at her like that?*

He narrowed his eyes as the deacon practically leaned into her pew with his tray, trying to get Tasha's attention. Jerome knew that there weren't that many single ladies at the church these days, but this man's behavior was too much. *All that ain't even necessary!*

Tasha scooted further away and avoided the man's leering eyes as she placed her offering onto the tray. The deacon, clearly forgetting where he was, must've not been happy with her stance toward him and nudged the tray closer to her. At this point, the deacon was about one nudge away from falling over.

Jerome's patience was almost gone, but before he could think of a way to intervene, Tasha stood up and squared off at the man. The deacon misread what was happening and grinned as Tasha marched toward him, though when she was within arm's length, instead of acknowledging or smiling at the man, she twirled further away from his reach and continued walking toward the front of the church stage.

The deacon's face fell, and Jerome almost laughed out loud as Tasha took a seat next to Evelyn. Whispers could be heard within the congregation as Evelyn smiled at Tasha and reached out to touch her mini side fade.

I guess no one saw her come in . . . Jerome felt the need to curse and found himself smiling. *Yeah, I may have been spending too much time with Tash these days.*

The deacons then all lined up towards the pit to hand their trays to the head deacon and Jerome kept his eye on the deacon from earlier. *If he even breathes wrong in front of Mama, he'll be meeting the Father today!*

As the Deacons turned their trays in, some of them would greet the first lady by bowing slightly toward her before taking their seats. He could see that Tasha was unaware of this, but as she observed the first few deacons do so, understanding kicked in and he noticed her posture straightened as her eyes lost their previous merriment from being near Evelyn. The pushy deacon from earlier was about to walk past them and Jerome narrowed his eyes. *Give me a reason man, I wish you would.*

The deacon kept his face neutral as he walked toward Evelyn to bow, though in his haste, he did not stop as he made a slight bow and tripped over his feet. Silence fell over the first few pews as he caught himself and all but sprinted back to his seat. Satisfied with the sight in front of him, Jerome relaxed a little into his seat as Senior took to the pit again.

"Today, I feel a calling to talk about false friends. Is that alright church?"

"Of course Pastor!"

Jerome finally looked toward Senior and did not like what he saw.

"You see, folks are known to come and go in your lives as the Lord sends them to you. But sometimes, he sends people as lessons and not true blessings!"

Nodding and clapping was heard throughout the congregation, but Jerome was now on high alert. *This was not the sermon that I saw him working on this Tuesday.*

"To learn and be of service to the Most High, trials and tribulations happen. That can come in the form of someone closest to you —even someone that you have come to call a friend!"

Senior pulled out his satin handkerchief and wiped his forehead as someone shouted, "Take yo time, Pastor!"

Jerome heard the projection screen behind him turn on and whipped his neck up to see someone upstairs in the AV room. *I don't like this, but I gotta stay cool,* Jerome reminded himself. *Senior could be trying some new material meant to connect to the younger members of the church.* It's not as if he's been on talking terms with the man since walking out weeks ago. So, he had to be patient and see where this goes. *Reserve opinions for later with a cool head, Rome.*

But once images of Tasha appeared on the projection screen, that notice sailed out of his head. Jerome bolted up from his seat, but before he could speak, Senior addressed the congregation again. "For months now, there has been a wolf donning sheep's clothing within our community. They have been persistent in poisoning my own flesh and blood against me. How can I possibly make their evil plans known and save my loved one, you ask?"

"Tell us, Pastor! What will you do?"

Jerome saw Tasha appear in front of the pit, staring hard at Senior. "Is there a reason you have me on your screen right now?" She spoke evenly, but her eyes must have sliced into the pastor's heart, as he backed away from her voice.

"You let that false friend know that you see them for who they truly are! You say to them, Jesus has shown me your heart! I know your true intent! Be gone from me, for you mean me no good!"

Tasha then took out her phone and snapped two photos, one of the screen and one of Senior. "I understand that you don't like me. Fine. But, as much as this will hurt your ego to hear, I ain't here for you. I'll ask again, why are there photos of me on this projector? Without my consent?"

"Where you work, you would know a bit about consent, uh?"

Hearing the Deacon's laugh sent Jerome over the edge. *Have these fools forgotten where they are right now?!* "That is enough!" Jerome shouted. Turning his attention to his Father, he finally spoke, "Why are you doing this? What has Tash done to provoke you so much?"

"You dare question me in MY HOUSE boy?!" The growl Senior released was loud enough to cause feedback into the microphone he held, which crackled throughout the building. Some folks covered their ears from the sound.

"Her feral wiles have blinded you that much? Well, that ends now, son! Eugene, play that footage."

Both Tasha and Jerome turned to the AV room and shouted almost in unison, "Don't you dare!"

"No!"

Tasha reached into her bag again, but this time she took out what Jerome thought looked like a fuzzy ball before clipping it onto her phone and plugging it into the usb port as she turned to face Senior again. "Since your cheap 'dirty dozen' clearly know where I work, let me make something that I learned from the BU very clear. You are in possession of a private recording of me, secured without my knowledge. All parties involved in the presenting of whatever is on this footage and playing it without my consent will hear from my legal counsel."

Evelyn finally stood up and looked at Senior. "Stop this now! This young woman is your son's friend! Why would you think otherwise?"

Senior ignored her and instead addressed Tasha, "I keep no counsel but the Father, the Son, and the Holy Ghost."

"That much is obvious, but not nan one of them will stop me from taking you to court."

Jerome saw the resolve in Tasha's eyes, and he looked at the screen again. *Wait, isn't that my living room?* He squinted and quickly widened his eyes after recognizing the scripture he'd painted on the main wall of his apartment. "How did you get this footage, Senior?" Jerome asked.

The entire congregation began buzzing at the informal way he addressed his daddy, but Jerome did not care. Walking down the small steps and standing next to Tasha, Jerome turned to look at Senior.

"Do you all see how busy the devil is at work? He has found a vessel that not only has poisoned my son against me, but the first lady as well!"

Tasha looked up at Jerome and whispered harshly, "I know he's your daddy, but I ain't gonna be one more devil or tainted vessel today."

Jerome nodded as Evelyn closed her eyes. The congregation was chatting again until the first lady spoke, "Jerome, this is not right. You putting this young woman on trial? For what? Things out of her control? For not bending to your will? Stop this now and talk to your son in private. Please!"

Tasha looked at Evelyn, and Jerome watched as she blinked her eyes and cautiously walked toward Evelyn to place a hand on her shoulder. "Mrs. Grant, I agree with what you are saying, but please do not get involved any further because of me. You're the first lady of Christ's Corner."

Evelyn looked at Tasha and smiled. "I know my place baby, and it is with my children. I forgot that once, and it cost me my first born. I will not make that mistake again today."

Hearing Evelyn mention Eva made Jerome's throat tighten. "Mama . . ." He went toward her and wrapped her in a bear hug. Once he let her go, Jerome saw the unshed tears in her eyes and felt his blood boil. But before his rage came out, Evelyn spoke to him.

"The Lord brought this woman into your life for a reason. Maybe just for a season or for the rest of your lives. But that is not for anyone in this room to decide besides the two of you." Turning to face Senior, Evelyn spoke again, "You will not take another child from me. If you play whatever you have on that there tape and cause this woman any more harm, you will find yourself without a home to come to when you leave this place today!"

Jerome and Tasha both looked on in shock as Evelyn went back to the pew, grabbed her purse, and marched down the aisle to leave.

Senior looked like he was going to be sick. Wiping his neck and forehead with his handkerchief, he closed his eyes tightly as everyone heard the echo of the main entrance doors creak open and snap shut. The congregation was silent, waiting to see what he would do next. Jerome hung his head and waited for the inevitable as Senior, never one to disappoint them, shouted to Eugene in AV, "Play that video NOW!"

TASHA

One Week Ago

Man, tonight was busier than this place has been in months! As she wiped down the counters in the food truck before locking up for the night, Tasha reached into her back pockets and grinned as her generous tips weighed down her denim jeans.

But that was not the only reason that she was in such high spirits. It had been a full seven days since she'd gotten to hang out with Rome, and they agreed to meet up later at his place. She could not wait to show him the surprise she had found for him earlier. *Flea Markets for the dang WIN!*

Just imagining the look on his face when she finally gave him a piece of his missing childhood put some extra pep in Tasha's step as she double checked to make sure everything was in its place before locking up. She was so caught up in her exit, Tasha almost didn't see Rookie and Patrick on the side of the club. When the two women locked eyes and Tasha saw the tears streaming down the younger girl's face, Tasha centered her feet before clenching her fists, as her eyes zeroed in on Patrick's chest in seconds.

"The club closed hours ago. Where is your gear and ride Rookie?"

Not waiting for a response, Tasha relaxed her jaw and hands before she took the ASP out of her side pocket and gripped it tightly. She stood only a few steps away from Patrick, who laughed.

Rookie waved her hands out in front of her face to get Tasha's attention. "Tash, e-everything is cool. I just had a rough night is all," Rookie tried to explain.

Tasha, not satisfied with that answer, pressed on. "With three bachelorette parties and a divorce entourage twenty folks deep, I knew that already. But don't none of that answer the question that I just asked you."

Patrick strolled up to Tasha, and she extended her arm, still holding the ASP, ready to release it if necessary. *Just give me a reason, you ashy son of a bitch!* she thought furiously.

"She left her gear inside, and I'm her new ride," he said, chuckling as if he were sharing some inside joke with friends.

Tasha's eyes narrowed on Patrick's before she glanced over to Rookie. She looked fine— well, as fine as could be expected wearing strappy high heels for eight hours straight. Wearing her street clothes and sporting her natural hair in a single French braid, Tasha wondered if Rookie was even old enough to be working at Bottom's Up. Tasha didn't like the idea of leaving the girl with this hotep, so she asked Rookie again, "You sure you don't have another ride? I am more than happy to take you home, sis."

Rookie looked up at her and smiled. "You sure you don't have a thing for me Tash?"

Thinking about the latest rumor among the girls from backstage, about how Tasha keeps the veggie items on the truck's menu because she was sweet on Rookie, Tasha smiled for a second with the girl. Patrick clearly didn't like being left out of the joke, as he grabbed Rookie's wrist and led her to the parking lot. "See, she's fine. Go eat some fries or something . . ."

Tasha frowned as she saw Rookie wince from his grip on her wrist. The two shared one last look as Patrick unlocked the car door and went to the driver's side to start the engine. She looked on as Rookie got inside and put on her seatbelt as Patrick sped out of the parking lot.

Why did I even bother? She grown, Tasha reminded herself as she walked to her car to leave.

She made it to Jerome's in hardly no time at all, and let herself in. "You really just left the door open?" she asked him in disbelief.

Seeing him come out of the kitchen wearing his old college t-shirt and ratty sweatpants did something funny to her heartstrings. Gripping the shopping bag in her hand to stop from reaching out for him, Tasha sat on the couch and put the shopping bag down.

"What? You texted me 30 minutes ago saying that you'd be here, so I unlocked the door while I was re-heating your meal."

That was a surprise change in conversation, and Tasha's growling stomach welcomed it. Inhaling deeply and closing her eyes in glee, she asked excitedly, "Rome, is that country fried chicken, cabbage, and rice? This late at night?"

He rubbed the back of his head and grinned. "Well, you said you missed having it since you moved out of your family's home. So when I went to see my folks, I asked Mama to help me make it for dinner today."

Tasha almost caught whiplash from turning to face Jerome after that admission. "Did you really?" she shrieked.

He nodded as he went back to the kitchen and came out with a well-plated serving of her favorite Sunday meal. Jerome set the plate down on the coffee table in front of her and dashed back into the kitchen to return with a mason jar of sweet iced tea. "You said that you only drink bottled water while at The Fast Fix, so I thought you would like this too."

Tasha's heart started doing that funny flippy flop thing again as she stared between her late night meal and Jerome. At that moment, she was more than a little frightened by the fact that she honestly didn't know which one she wanted more. Clearing her throat, Tasha sat down on the floor and picked up her fork to taste the meal he had made for her. The steak was fried well; it was a little too peppery for her liking, but still good. Sighing, she then picked up the mason jar and almost drank the entire serving of sweet tea in one go. "Did you make the tea too?" She asked.

Chuckling lightly, Jerome lowered his eyes. "Well, I had a full day of preparing this meal with Mama, so I stopped by the bodega on the corner to pick up the tea."

Tasha let herself imagine for a second too long coming home to something like this years from now, and it was enough to send slight palpitations to her heart. "Thank you Rome. This was really sweet of you," she told him softly.

"You're welcome."

She ate in silence for a few more minutes as Jerome returned to the kitchen to clean up. While he was there, Tasha took out her surprise for him and made quick work of her meal before he came out into the living room again. Just as she placed her now empty plate and glass on his small kitchenette table, Tasha was rewarded to seeing the sight of this grown man jumping up and down like it was Christmas morning.

"Tash! Wh-where did you find this?" he asked her excitedly.

"At the flea market just outside of town. I didn't want to tell you until I could test it out and make sure it still worked."

He hopped on the couch and grabbed a game controller as he took in all the games that Tasha had found for the console.

"I just thought you should have as many gaming sets as you can. You know, to make up for not getting to play these as a jit. It's no big deal, really."

Jerome leaped out of his seat, and she thought his face would crack if he kept smiling that widely at her. "Thank you, Tash. This is just—thank you," he finished awkwardly.

"You're welcome. Do you want to play a game now?"

"Fo sho! Let's plug it up already!"

She sat on the couch again and watched as Jerome buzzed around his living room, taking care to put each cord in place for the new gaming system before turning on the TV and pressing start on the small black box. As the gaming music started, even Tasha was giddy with the thought of playing. "Are you ready to be schooled Rome?"

Jerome looked at her and laughed "I see you's a trash talker when it comes to gaming, uh?"

They shared a laugh again as the two began the arcade-style fighting game. Hours passed, and even though Tasha didn't have to work the next day, she wanted to get some sleep. But she was enjoying watching Jerome concentrate on the different tasks and getting to higher levels of the game too much to say anything. *Besides, I remember what it was like for me playing this game coming up. Me and Tina would stay up until four or five am playing.* She thought back on the memory and felt her eyes well up. Before she could get too into her feelings, Tasha got up from the couch and went to the linen closet to grab her pillow and sheets. As she was turning the corner to go back to the living room, she noticed that Jerome's bedroom door was open.

Curiosity was a dangerous thing.

Tasha had been avoiding this room for weeks, and Jerome never left the door open. So of course she now found herself wanting to see what was in there. The small justifications started in her mind, one after another. *He wouldn't mind if I took a peek . . . I'll just glance around inside as I close the door . . .*

Thankfully, someone above was looking out for her as Jerome called her name, bringing Tasha back to her senses. Quickly walking back into the living room with her bedding and pillows, Tasha began to set up camp for the night. "What's up?" she asked.

Jerome was in her face seconds after pausing the game. "This level is a beast! Do you have any tips on how to beat the final boss on this round?"

The excitement on his face was too adorable for words, so Tasha brought her attention to the screen and offered a few suggestions before Jerome flopped down on the floor and she snuggled deeper into the couch. The last thing she remembered was hearing Jerome's shouts of victory as he finally beat the main boss.

TASHA SLOWLY ROSE FROM the couch to look around. Both gaming systems and their controllers were nestled away into an old shoe box. Seeing that made a groggy Tasha giggle, though she sounded more like a frog when she did so, getting Jerome's attention.

"Ah, shoot, my bad. I didn't mean to wake you," he said.

Tasha shook her head and blinked a few times before she spoke. "It's okay. You didn't wake me up." Tasha became more alert and could smell something burnt. It must've shown on her face, as Jerome shyly told her about his morning.

"Well, last night you really liked the dinner that I made you. So I thought maybe I could make you waffles for breakfast . . . as a thank you for the gaming gear."

She looked his way pleasantly, and an idea formed in her head. Before she lost her nerve, Tasha asked Jerome bluntly, "Why don't we just go to Wayward Waffles then?"

It was Jerome's turn to stare at her.

"For real?" he asked.

Tasha nodded and headed to the bathroom to shower and change into her street clothes. By the time she had finished up, Jerome had straightened up the living room and the kitchen before disappearing. She called him until she realized that there was only one place he could be in at the moment.

Should I knock on his door? she wondered. She'd won the battle last night, but curiosity was well on its way to winning the war as Tasha quietly made her way to his closed bedroom door. Knocking tentatively, she waited for him to respond. Jerome cracked the door open and Tasha's eyes were treated to a glimpse of his broad shoulders and thick bare thighs as he stuck his head out.

"I'll be out in just a few minutes, okay?" he told her quickly.

"Okay." *We're only going to Waywards. Why is Jerome making such a big deal?*

When Jerome finally stepped into the living room and grabbed his keys, Tasha realized too late why he was bugging. This would be their first public outing together. *Shit!*

Yeah, they had traveled to the beach when the truck needed repairing and Tasha was given time off from working outside the club, but that was at least three hours away. And she was not sure what to make of their relationship lately. Are they friends? Or is this becoming something else?

From the way Jerome was dressed, it was safe to say that they were on their way to becoming more than just friends. His outfit didn't exactly match her royal blue romper, but the white linen shorts and blue t-shirt that had 'Try Jesus' written in white and black script did complement her attire just a little too well. She could smell faint notes of his woodsy cologne, and it mixed harmoniously with the vanilla and almond body wash from her morning shower.

Anyone would instantly think we were a couple when they saw us together. She thought nervously.

"Okay. You ready to get your grub on? My treat?"

Tasha gulped. *Yeah, there was no mistaking it now. This for sure counts as their first date.*

Jerome
Present Day, Sunday

The congregation was silent as they saw Jerome bring Tasha a plate of food on the recording. Soon someone shouted up to the AV room, "Where is the sound?"

He could see a few members of the church move from their pews in the back rows to the front ones. And even though Jerome knew that right now everyone's eyes were watching him, he couldn't wipe the smile off his face. *After that night, she asked me out.* He remembered smugly. Well, technically, as he found out later, Tasha wasn't really asking him out. But when she suggested they have breakfast at an actual restaurant and not in their night clothes as they normally would have, Jerome thought of the occasion as a date and dressed the part.

Hearing more mumbles from the pews, Jerome went back to the screen and had to look away from the embarrassment, as he could then be seen jumping up and down with joy on the screen. *I really did that, uh?*

He winced as he heard Tasha try not to laugh, but once he turned to fully look at her, she lost it and let out a loud snort in front of everyone. The screen now showed her throwing up her hands and getting in his face after she had beaten the first main boss from the arcade fighting game. Jerome found himself chuckling alongside her before the screen went blue and cut off completely.

The murmurs grew louder in the pews, and Jerome thought Senior was going to faint as he lurched over the podium. Tasha rounded on him, but before she spoke, Jerome laid a gentle hand on her wrist to get her attention. Seeing her eyes soften, he removed his hand and stepped down from the stage as he got comfortable in the first pew.

"I do not want to know what you thought you were going to expose me for with this stunt you just tried to pull, but since it is you that seems to be the one suffering any real embarrassment, I won't involve my attorney with this. Next time, I will call them down here to take statements, that I promise you."

"You still everything he said - false friend!" one deacon shouted. Tasha's head whipped around to the sound, but Jerome was up and in action before she could speak.

"Let him who is without sin among you be the first to throw a stone at her. John 8:7."

Jerome's glare intensified toward Patrick, causing the man to blink several times before Jerome added, "And why you thought it would be okay to attack a woman in this place is beyond me, but it ain't gonna go down like that today!" His chest rose and fell as he shouted at his former friend. Now it was Tasha's turn to calm him down as she stepped away from the front of the stage and grabbed his hand.

"Let's just go, Rome. Let it go."

He stared hard at her and all but growled, "It was bad enough when Senior was coming for you, but now this fool's got something to say too? Tash, I can't sit on this no more!"

She blocked him from getting in Patrick's face by putting both of her hands on his chest.

"I get it, trust me, I do. And normally, I would be first to sit back and let y'all brawl, but Rome, this ain't the time or place. Let's go. Please."

Feeling the heat from Patrick's disrespect and the deacon from earlier had Jerome ready to box, for sure, but then Tasha said something that made him pause.

"You asked me once how I can find joy in my life with all that I have had to deal with. I'll tell you: I make a choice. Every day, I choose happiness! I choose peace! Will beating this chump's ass bring you either of those things?"

Jerome paused to look at her. Tasha's face was stern, but in those deep brown eyes he saw the truth. She was right. Yeah, while choking out Patrick in the nearest pew would feel good for a minute, once it was done, he would regret it. Not the laying hands part, but the laying hands in a place of worship part. Still too angry to speak, but hearing her words, Jerome hung his head and let Tasha lead them down the pews until they were in the church lobby.

As she reached for the door handle, Jerome pulled Tasha close, wrapping one of his hands around her waist and bringing her back into his chest. At first Tasha tensed up from his touch, but soon she dropped her hand from the handle and let Jerome rest his head on her shoulder as she placed her hand over his while he held her close. Feeling her relax under his touch did things to Jerome's spirit that even he didn't think was possible. To know that this woman, who has endured so much, trusted him enough to allow him to seek solace in her embrace . . . he could spend the rest of his life trying to explain that feeling and never come close. "Thank you," Jerome softly whispered before letting her go.

She opened the door and the sunlight greeted them both while holding hands and walking out of Christ's Corner's doors. "Let's check in on your mama, okay?"

THE TWO OF THEM COULD smell the Sunday meal as they exited the car, and Tasha let Jerome lead the way as they entered the house. Evelyn's favorite gospel singers could be heard on her small radio in the kitchen, so that is where Jerome headed first. Seeing his mother chopping greens over the kitchen sink, shame rolled off of him in waves. Instead of trying to box with Patrick in church, he realized that they should have just come here. In between cutting the greens, Evelyn sniffled and wiped her face with the back of her hand. Jerome looked back at Tasha, who was also blinking back tears. *They've only known each other for a few weeks and their bond was already that strong?* he thought to himself as he slowly approached his mother and placed a hand on her shoulder.

She stopped cutting, letting the board and knife fall into the bowl in the sink as she turned around and wrapped her arms around him. "My baby! You came home!" she shouted as tears fell down her cheeks.

"Yes ma'am. Tash said we needed to, um, check on you after you left."

His mother then looked over him and saw Tasha hiding quietly in the doorway to the kitchen. "Chile, I ain't gonna hurt you! What you doing hanging onto the doorway?" Waving Tasha over with her hands, Evelyn took her time looking her over before asking, "Did he play that tape of you, baby?"

Tasha looked Evelyn in the eye as she answered, "Yes, ma'am." Seeing Evelyn's eyes narrow as she gripped her apron, Jerome was glad that his father was not there at that moment.

"That dang fool! He just couldn't help himself!" Evelyn shouted again as she took off her apron and tossed it on the counter. She then walked to the dinner table and plopped down in the front chair.

Tasha kneeled down in front of Evelyn and took one of her hands inside her own. "Mrs. Grant, I'm alright. Please don't let what happened today cause you any more stress. Besides, the video exposé did not go down as Pastor Grant thought it would.``

Seeing the edges of Tasha's lips curl up despite her best efforts to make them stop got Evelyn's attention. "Baby, what do you mean?" Evelyn asked, now full of curiosity.

Tasha bit back a laugh as Jerome sat next to his mother to explain. "Well, in the video, Tash and I were playing a video game and I was losing. Badly. So Tash started being very unsportsmanlike and started saying a bunch of unladylike things at me." Evelyn looked between the two of them, surprise written all over her face as Jerome continued, "But the thing is, no one heard any of it, because there was no sound during the video."

Tasha snorted as she stood up, and Jerome rolled his eyes. "Really Tash? You still think it's funny to kick a man when he's down?" he asked her, completely serious.

"Yes! You really thought you could beat me at a game you never played and had the nerve to be shocked when you didn't!" Her giggles bounced off the walls in the kitchen, and Jerome watched as his mother stared at the two of them. He just knew any minute now she was going to ask him something that he didn't want to answer . . .

And he was right.

"So, you have been spending the night at my son's home . . . playing video games?"

Her tone told him just how shocked she was by this news and Tasha, without thinking, answered. "Yes ma'am! Why—" Realization came tumbling around her like a bag of bricks and Jerome would have laughed at the look on her face if it wasn't his mama asking this question. Her cheeks turned the faintest shade of blush, and Tasha's eyes quickly went to the floor.

"Do you want us to help you finish making dinner, Mama?" Jerome asked.

Soon, the three of them were sitting around the table to a hearty meal of collard greens, rice, black-eyed peas, and cornbread. Tasha took another sip of her lemonade before she raised her glass. "Mrs. Grant, this is so good! Thank you!"

"You welcome baby. Stop by anytime you want a home-cooked meal, okay?"

Tasha nodded excitedly as she took another bite of her cornbread. Jerome watched the women in his life enjoying this meal together, and he thought of this becoming their new tradition a year from now, though in his mind Tasha was wearing an engagement ring. The thought wouldn't leave his mind, even as he rejoined their conversation about the upcoming holidays. *If I ask her now, I know she will say no.* He tried to let the thought go as he went back to enjoying the moment in front of him. After helping Evelyn clean up and her giving them both leftovers from their meal, Jerome and Tasha drove in silence back to his place.

She'll be making her way home soon. He told himself, even though he didn't want her to leave. That is really what he learned today through all the mess that went down at church. Jerome wanted Tasha to remain a constant in his life. Maybe a few months of being just friends was too soon to ask her what was on his mind, but his heart had been ready to do just that for a while now. He may not have had much experience in this romance thing, but Jerome could sense that he wasn't all alone in his feelings these days. Knowing that only made him want to ask her even more.

"Rejoice in hope, be patient in tribulation, be constant in prayer," he reminded himself. Letting Tasha enter the apartment first, he heard her yawn and watched as she headed to the bathroom. Soon he could hear water running in the bathroom and Jerome went still. Soon Tasha emerged from the bathroom wearing a fresh pair of night pajamas. Jerome wanted to stop and worship to the most high to give thanks for answering his prayer that she would stay over just one more night. Trying to be cool about this surprise development, Jerome jokingly asked, "Did you leave me any hot water?"

Tasha sucked her teeth. "I wasn't in there that long, big head!"

He said nothing as he walked past her toward his room. Even though it was still early, just half-past eight o'clock, Jerome took a shower and brushed his teeth before joining an already sleepy-looking Tasha on the couch. "So today was wild."

She nodded, seemingly too tired to talk. "I'm just glad you're okay," Tasha said.

Not expecting that response, and now curious, Jerome had to ask, "What do you mean?"

She turned to look at him, surprised that he had to ask. "What if what your daddy thought was on that video was in fact really on that tape? Can you imagine? The whole church would have seen you and me getting sweaty!" Jerome's ears were on fire as he listened to Tasha weakly giggle out loud. "We haven't once talked about our relationship, and it seems like everyone—including your Mama—thought it was more than what it was. Why is that?" she wondered out loud.

Jerome knew that the possibility of having this conversation again was slim, so he took a chance and went for it. "I want to be more than friends with you, Tasha." This got her attention, as Tasha held his gaze. "Maybe everyone can see that, except you?" Jerome continued.

Tasha let out a deep yawn, and Jerome reached out to trace the outline of her jaw. She smiled, and he wanted to commit that to his memory too, so he brought his thumb toward the outline of her lips before he felt her freeze under his touch. "Jerome . . ." she whispered.

He stopped for a second to look up into Tasha's eyes. The two of them have been this close before, but that usually involved them playing video games or laughing hard at one another's jokes. Jerome felt the atmosphere change as he held her gaze. Seeing Tasha briefly close her eyes, Jerome ran his index finger over her other features as well. He noted her smooth forehead, the light textures just under her eyebrows and how the lower end of her nose pointed down, drawing more attention to her full lips. As he was trying to capture the exact roundness of her cheeks, Tasha spoke again, "You and I are friends - good friends. But just friends."

Not ready to let go of where this conversation could lead, Jerome asked her while he brought his fingertips back under her jaw, "Do you think, in time, that we could become more than friends?"

Hearing a small inhale and exhale, Jerome waited for her to answer his question. "Any woman would be lucky to have you as a partner, Rome." That wasn't what he asked, so he repeated the question. This time, he gently placed his fingertips behind Tasha's ear and was rewarded to the sound of her releasing a sharp inhale of breath. Tasha grabbed his hand.

"Yes, okay?"

Removing his hand from her ear, Jerome trailed his fingers back down to the sides of her face before asking another question. "Where do you see our relationship going now?"

"Somewhere that I didn't prepare for at all, and that scares me."

His breath now shallow from her admission, Jerome knew he was being greedy when he asked, "What does your wedding day look like?"

Her eyes slowly opened, and he met them. "I never really saw myself getting married. But if I did, I know it would be a small gathering. Maybe ten to twenty people. I would want to have the ceremony somewhere outside, and I would for sure not walk down the aisle to that tired-ass wedding march song."

He smiled as he made a mental note of everything she just shared. "What song would you want to meet your future husband down the aisle to then?" Jerome asked gently.

Tasha thought the question over and her answer left him with a burning knot in his throat.

"I don't know the name of the original song, but the one that you sampled for the last track to your EP? The ballad one? Yeah, I could see myself walking down the aisle to a track like that."

Before he could stop himself, Jerome brought his face inches away from hers. "Really? You liked 'Here on Paradise' that much?"

Tasha nodded, and Jerome dropped his hand from her face and brought his forehead toward hers. There was only breathing room between them, and Jerome thought it was too much as he leaned in closer. Their lips touched, and he wanted to never go another day without feeling the softness of her lips against his.

"Please stop."

He didn't want to make her feel uncomfortable, so Jerome backed up a bit and saw that her eyes were still closed. Smiling, he asked one more question. "Who do you see waiting for you at the end of the aisle?"

Tasha shook her head. "I've answered enough of your questions for one night. Go to bed," she told him flatly as she tried to hide another yawn.

Chucking softly at her stubbornness, Jerome stood up and went to his room.

Chapter Seven
Season's Greetings

asha

T   She woke up well before her alarm and knew it was time to go. The sun wasn't even out yet, but Tasha made quick work of picking up all her things from around Jerome's place and calling a ride share to drop her off outside of Christ's Corner. The entire way home, all she could think about was the kiss they shared. By the time she made it home, Tasha knew she could not spend the night at his place.

When Jerome kissed her last night, she wanted to finally see what the inside of his room looked like—as she laid in bed with him. And there was no way she would let the two of them go from being just friends and constantly avoiding talking about becoming something more, to skating around talks of a wedding straight to making his headboard creak. As much as she wanted to, Tasha would not let that happen. *No more sleepovers. Not even a late-night visit*, she vowed.

Before Jerome could tempt her with another home cooked meal or a new game to play, Tasha typed up a text:

I think we should put a stop to the sleepovers for now.
With everything that just went down. Okay?
- Tash

Tasha stared at the message for a second before she hit send. Putting her phone on silent, she got into photography mode for the day. Firing up her computer and inserting her SD card reader, Tasha looked over the photos that she and Jerome took when they went to Bejon Beach.

As she heard her roomies wake up and start their day, Tasha was finishing up the edits on the photos that Jerome had taken. Overall, the photos really were good; she had little to no editing to do on most of them. After she had created a separate new folder to place them in, Tasha got up to stretch and say hi to the girls. She saw Alexa first, sitting on the couch, still in her pajamas as Rachel brought out a breakfast tray of food.

"You two are too cute!" Tasha said brightly, getting their attention.

Rachel beamed as Alexa kissed her cheek. "What brings you here at this hour?" Rachel asked Tasha cheerfully.

Thankful that she didn't have to lie again, Tasha smiled. "I wanted to finish up some edits and see you two bums. But if y'all are busy I can—"

"Nah, come here, homie! We ain't seen you in a minute," Alexa said as Rachel waved Tasha over to join them.

Tasha squeezed in on the couch with them and started watching their latest reality TV show marathon. Curious, she asked, "Is this how you two spend your days off?"

Alexa laughed as Rachel turned to answer, "Yes sis! Don't judge!"

Tasha put her hands out in front of her face. "No judgment! Just wondering, is all."

"When you're with the one you love, moments like these, where you unwind from everything the world has thrown at you, are the best," Alexa told Tasha before peppering Rachel with more kisses. It warmed Tasha's heart seeing her close friends still in love after so many years together.

"Why you want to know? You feeling something for ole boy Jerome?" Rachel asked her directly.

Caught off guard, Tasha looked at her two friends and pressed her lips together. *How can I get out of this one?* She thought quickly.

Apparently, Tasha took too long to answer, and both of the women began whooping and hollering. "I knew it was only a matter of time! Babe, look at her face!" Rachel said as she hugged Alexa, who looked at Tasha with a twinkle in her eyes.

"Yeah, I know that look. That's definitely love," she confirmed.

Tasha hadn't even said the words to Jerome yet, and here were her closest friends, making her finally confront what she had been feeling for weeks now. Knowing that it was time for her to admit the truth, Tasha looked at them hopefully as she asked softly, "Is it that obvious?" Alexa and Rachel looked at one another as Alexa pushed their breakfast tray away. The two then engulf Tasha in a hug. As they separated, Tasha sighed, "I just don't want things to get weird between us!"

Rachel rubbed Tasha's back as Alexa spoke. "So don't let them! Tell him how you feel and see what he says."

Tasha wasn't a fool. She knew where Jerome was going with his line of questioning the other night. But that was a leap she wasn't ready for just yet. Telling him how she felt was hard enough, but she knew Alexa was right. "I'm scared," Tasha finally admitted. "Y'all have seen the dudes Trish gets involved with, and I strongly doubt any of the women in my family have ever had a serious relationship. What if I mess up my friendship with Rome by trying to be his girl?"

Rachel looked at Alexa and then at Tasha. "Love is scary sis, but it's worth the risk." She looked on as Rachel kissed Alexa's cheek and the two shared another brief peck on the lips. "Tell him Tash," Rachel urged her gently.

Looking at both of her friends, Tasha nodded slowly. "Okay."

JEROME

He knew he had gone too far with all the questions the other night, as he woke up to Tasha's text the next morning. When Jerome finally dragged himself out of bed, he noticed that all her things were also gone, and he wanted to kick himself for being so persistent.

Getting ready for a day of volunteering at the center, Jerome tried to not think about it too much and focused on enrolling students into ASL class for the new semester at the office. Betty, a CODA and his manager, waved him over after Jerome finished helping two women choose between a few beginner ASL learner course books.

"How's it going today, Jerome?" She asked him brightly.

"It's going okay. Busy."

"That's expected, with Thanksgiving right around the corner. I just wanted to let you know that the office will be closed all next week. Can we count on seeing you again in December?"

Jerome forced a smile to his face as he nodded. "Yeah, I'll see you then."

Betty smiled at him again as she walked away. "You'll be locking up with James this evening, so make sure he doesn't keep you too long today, okay?"

Jerome waved at her and sighed. He should have known that the center would close soon for the holidays, but with everything that had happened at church recently, Jerome was just happy to have somewhere else to be beside Christ's Corner. And as much as he loved his mother, the cold shoulder from his father was getting to be too much. Senior hardly said more than a few words at a time to him these days, and Jerome didn't know what to do. He thought back to his talk with Tasha and how he had tried to apologize for any disrespect he may have caused over the last two weeks, but Senior shut him down almost immediately. Jerome remembered seeing the look on his mother's face as she went to him after his attempt.

There was no way he would do that again. Part of him wanted to see if he could get his mama to come to his place for Thanksgiving, but Jerome knew she would never leave Senior to fend for himself. The day passed on and before he knew it, the center was closing. The other volunteer, James, rushed around to the counter, whistling happily. Jerome looked at him, envious of his good mood, and said goodnight.

After he made it home and showered, Jerome pressed one on this phone and waited for Evelyn to answer her phone.

"Hey baby! How was your day?"

"It was good. But I was thinking . . . would it be alright if I stayed home next week instead of stopping by for Thanksgiving?"

Jerome heard Mama shuffle around before she whispered harshly into the other end of the phone. "Jerome Earl Grant Junior! Now I know things have not been easy between you and your daddy, but don't you dare think about not coming home for Thanksgiving!"

He knew that would be her response, but Jerome had to try. Sighing, he asked sincerely, "What else can I do, Mama? He won't even talk to me when I am there, and at church he act like I'm invisible."

The line was silent for a minute before Evelyn made a suggestion. "Well, if he won't talk to you, bring someone with you who will."

Jerome sat upright. "Mama! Do you mean . . ."

She whispered again. "Yes! Invite Tasha and let's get all of this out in the open now. The way we should have from the very beginning!"

Jerome didn't want to put Tasha through any more of his family's mess, but he could hear the strain in his mother's voice. He knew all of this must have been hard on her too.

"Yes ma'am. I will ask her today," Jerome promised. "I love you Mama," he added before ending their call. Jerome then looked at his phone again and pressed number two. Eva picked up on the third ring, and Jerome sat up so she could see him signing during their talk. "I know it's been too long, but I need some big sisterly advice."

Eva grinned as she signed back, "Is this about the woman you told me about last time?" Jerome nodded.

"Are you ready to tell her how you feel?" Eva signed.

Jerome looked down briefly before signing to the screen. "Mama wants me to invite her over for Thanksgiving," he signed slowly, making sure to get each word right.

Eva blinked several times before signing back. "Let me know how it goes 'big head,'" she spelled out the last two words and Jerome laughed.

"Now tell me, how is life in New York these days?" he asked. They talked for a few more minutes before he heard his niece come into the room. Evelyn Mae was not so little anymore, and Jerome wished he could be there to see her grow up. Soon little Lyn's face was on the screen too, and she waved to Jerome. He waved back before saying goodbye.

With both Mama and Eva in agreement, Jerome called Tasha and asked her to be his plus one at his folks' place the following week.

———— ⚬⚬⚬ ————

EVELYN

While her husband walked around in his night clothes, Evelyn was prepping for a small feast. She wanted everything to go well and, to be honest, cooking was a great distraction from Senior's sour mood these days. After everything that happened at the church a few weeks ago, Evelyn thought her husband and son would mend their fences and at least be cordial toward each other. Her baby even made a genuine effort for peace, one that Jerome Senior shut down immediately. But today she had hope. Everyone was going to be on their best behavior and talk things out once and for all! Making sure to get the turkey seasoned well before putting it in the oven, Evelyn smiled brightly at her husband as she saw him finally dressed for the day. To thank him for the effort, she walked over and kissed him firmly on the lips. "How many sweet potato pies will you and Junior eat this year?" She called out to him as he went to watch football on the couch.

"As many as your lovely hands can make!" he shouted over the sound of the TV.

Evelyn blinked back tears as his familiar saying gave her hope.

TASHA

Throwing her fifth outfit idea onto her bed, Tasha was almost in tears as she tried to find an appropriate dress for Thanksgiving with Jerome's parents. She plopped back onto the bed in her bra and matching boy shorts and deeply sighed.

Tasha knew why she was nervous, but that didn't make her any calmer. It had been almost two weeks since she sent Jerome that text and she'd regretted it ever since. She missed going to his place after working at The Fast Fix, especially on busy nights. A few times Tasha went on autopilot as she began driving to his apartment, only to come to her senses halfway there and have to turn around. The worst of it all was his unbothered attitude after she sent him the text. Jerome never once tried to change Tasha's mind. He still called her every other day and even stopped by the apartment last week to have dinner with her and her roommates before they left to spend the holiday with Rachel's dad. She wanted to be mad at him, but really Tasha was upset with herself for how much she missed him. So after he called to ask her to spend Thanksgiving with him, Tasha agreed as soon as the words left his mouth. Which is why she couldn't take it back when he told her that that also meant they'd be having dinner with his parents.

Tasha had imagined them having Chinese food and maybe snuggling up on his couch to watch one of these cheesy 80's action movies that Jerome liked so much. But, oh no, the Lord decided to test her first with a dinner that put Senior Grant at the head of the table. And that is why Tasha found herself now on the struggle bus with choosing a dress the old hound couldn't judge her too harshly for wearing to his house.

Hearing her phone dinged, Tasha knew it was Jerome before she even looked at the screen.

Leaving the house now to pick up a few things for Mama.
See you in 20 minutes.

-Rome

Tasha tossed her phone behind her as she grabbed the nearest pillow to scream into. Sitting up again, she looked to her left and snatched up the purple dress. It was almost knee length and had a modest scoop neck top, so Tasha figured even Senior would struggle to find fault with it. Picking up her smaller messenger bag and throwing in her baby DSLR, along with a few other things, Tasha turned off the lights in her apartment and waited downstairs for Jerome to arrive.

She didn't miss the frown on his face as he pulled into the gated community, but Tasha was already too wired to consider his gentleman etiquette. Jerome stopped the car, and she sighed as he rushed to get out and open the passenger side door to let Tasha step inside. Leaning over to open his door before putting on her seatbelt, Tasha waited for him to drive before speaking. "You look nice," she said sweetly. He did. Even in his dark slacks and button collar shirt, Jerome looked like the star of a men's magazine spread. Tasha saw him look at her from the rearview mirror and smiled. "So, how long do these dinners usually last?" Tasha asked as they came to a stop sign.

Jerome looked at her apologetically and reached out for her hand. Tasha gave it to him eagerly, and he gave it a squeeze. Her heartbeat slowed down as she briefly looked into his eyes.

"Everything will be fine, I promise, okay?" Jerome tried to assure her while driving down the empty road.

Tasha felt her nerves rise again and the real reason she was a hot mess came rushing out of her mouth. "I want to be more than friends too, Rome. I mean, if I'm going to be having dinner with your folks, don't you think we should at least give our status a boost first?" Tasha finished breathlessly.

The car came to a halt after she finished speaking. Looking behind him, Jerome drove in reverse until they were inside an empty parking lot. "You mean it? You really want to go together now?" he asked her excitedly.

"Yeah, I do."

Jerome lifted her hand up to his lips and pressed down softly.

AS THEY PULLED UP TO Jerome's parents' house, Tasha twirled the strap to her small messenger bag tightly. She still couldn't believe that she agreed to this, and all Tasha could do as Jerome opened her car door was to send a rushed prayer to the OG above to not let her snap on Senior and ruin this dinner. The two walked up to the door, but before Jerome let himself in with his house key, he turned to Tasha and cupped her face into his hands. "Thank you for coming, Tash," he whispered before leaning down to press his lips against her forehead.

Tasha closed her eyes and soaked up his touch and she then heard him chuckling. Blinking quickly, she focused her sights on Jerome.

"What's so funny?"

"Nothing. I just like seeing your face after I kiss you is all," Jerome replied too smoothly for her liking.

Tasha didn't have a chance to say what she was thinking, as the door opened and she got a whiff of the small feast Evelyn Grant had been working on that day. The smell of collard greens mixed with something cinnamon-y and sweet had managed to lower her defenses as Jerome led her towards his father, which would explain the look of surprise on his face as she offered him a genuine smile. "Happy Thanksgiving Mr. Grant."

The older man looked between her and Jerome as he stammered out, "H-hello Ms. Daye."

Tasha wondered how long he would keep that formality up as she nodded and made her way into the kitchen. She watched from the door frame as Evelyn, clearly in her zone, took the most delectable ham Tasha had ever seen out of the oven and poked at what looked like cornbread dressing before closing the oven. The older woman finally noticed Tasha and sent a grin her way.

"If you don't quit hanging out over there and give me a hug, baby girl! I know something!"

Tasha went to do as Evelyn asked. Wrapping her arms around the woman tightly, Tasha closed her eyes for a second time that day as she swayed back and forth in the older woman's embrace. "Thank you for inviting me," Tasha said to her softly before staring down at the floor.

Evelyn lightly tapped her chin to bring Tasha's eyes up to hers. "Now, I know you worried, but there ain't no need to be. Senior may run things at Christ's Corner, but I run things up in here!"

The two laughed as Evelyn continued, "It is time to get everything out in the open once and for all. So don't you be scared, okay baby girl?"

Tasha nodded again as Evelyn reached for her hands and held them together tightly inside her own. Fighting the stinging around her eyes, Tasha cleared her throat. "Can I help with anything?"

Evelyn smiled, "Now that's what I'm talking about! Gone and put that apron on over there before you set that ham and turkey on the table."

THE TWO WOMEN FINALLY finish setting up the table, and Tasha's stomach dropped when Evelyn called both Jeromes to the kitchen table. Her Jerome came in first and motioned for Tasha to turn around. As he untied the apron from around her waist, she tried not to get distracted by the feel of his breath on her neck.

"Thank you for helping mama today. She loves celebrating this time of year," Jerome said as he folded the apron and went into the kitchen to put it away. Tasha followed him and as he turned around to go back to the table, she put her hands against his chest, pushing him into the corner of the kitchen.

"No thanks needed," she said before tilting her head up to kiss Jerome quickly on the lips.

Seeing him stare at her afterwards, touching his lips, Tasha smirked before going to sit at the dining room table.

Mr. Grant wasted no time leading everyone into prayer over the food as he held his hands out for his wife and Jerome. As he prayed, Tasha felt Jerome gently message her left hand. She knew he was trying to comfort her, though Jerome was doing more than he realized. Weeks of being away from him, even though it was by choice, had her ready to snatch his hand away and drag him back into the kitchen corner. Now that they were officially dating, Tasha wanted to touch him, well, all the time. But those aren't really thoughts you should be having about your boyfriend as his father said grace, so Tasha said another silent prayer to the OG that day to grant her some of the same self-control that they seem to have on unlimited supply for Jerome when she spent the night at his place all those weeks ago.

As grace ended, Tasha opened her eyes and smiled at Jerome before sitting. The food was slowly piling up on her plate and Tasha wasn't sure if she would be able to eat as much as her eyes told her she could.

"Tasha, baby, how are things going for you with your photography?" Evelyn asked.

Looking over at the woman, Tasha's eyes widened. "You know about my photography work?"

Her Jerome explained," I told Mama about it when she saw me looking at your online gallery from my phone a few days ago."

Tasha wanted to kiss him again as he blushed from the admission, and it must've shown because Mr. Grant finally spoke. "How do you find the time, Ms. Daye? Between working those late nights and staying up all hours with my son?" The older man coughed as he reached for his drink, and his wife showed her disappointment at him openly.

Tasha looked at Pastor Grant and waited for him to meet her stare before she answered his question. "Working at The Fast Fix allows me more time to focus on my photography during the weekday. And now that I am no longer tutoring at Christ's Corner, I have even more time to work on honing my craft."

She felt Jerome reach out for her hand again, but Tasha pulled hers away as she turned to smile at Senior. "Thank you for helping me finally make the leap into being a photographer full time," she told Mr. Grant sincerely.

Evelyn clapped her hands together excitedly. "That is good news, baby girl! Maybe someday we can see your work somewhere downtown."

"I'm sure if we go to one of them lewd sites-"

Jerome spoke this time, interrupting Senior, "Maybe one day folks can see the photos she's taken of me."

Tasha watched as both of his parents stared at him. "Jerome! What pictures are you talking about?" his father demanded.

Evelyn added, "You haven't posed in front of a camera since your college graduation photos!"

Jerome looked at Tasha and grinned. "Can I show them?"

"They're your photos. Do what you want, Rome."

He quickly got up from the table and went to get Tasha's bag from the kitchen. Jerome almost looked like a pro as he opened her bag and gently took her camera from its padded bag and turned it on. "We took these down at Bejon Beach a while ago," he explained as he handed the camera to his mother to look through. Hearing her gasp made Tasha feel like she was walking on air.

"Baby girl! These are just . . . just beautiful!"

Senior stood up and walked behind his wife to see the photos, and the two wordlessly looked through the reel.

"There aren't any, umm, you know?" Jerome whispered as he wiggled his eyebrows at Tasha.

She snorted before answering, "No. I wouldn't shoot those kinds of pictures with the daily cam."

Jerome grinned as Tasha held his hand under the table. So lost in gazing at one another, they both jumped as Evelyn cleared her throat to get their attention. They turned to look at her sheepishly as Evelyn smiled knowingly their way. Jerome stood to take the camera back from his mother and return it to Tasha's bag.

"I want a copy of each of them pictures," Evelyn told Tasha sternly. Tasha nodded as they all went back to enjoying their meal.

After eating, Jerome and Tasha went to the kitchen to clean up. The two worked silently for some time as Evelyn turned on the radio. Tasha hummed along to the Christmas music now playing in the background.

"Can we stay a little longer to help Mama put up the tree?"

Tasha turned to look at him. "Yeah, big head. Why would you even ask?"

Jerome put the last pot on the drying rack as he avoided her stare. "I thought it might be too much for you today, since you ain't going to see your family. And I don't want you to feel obligated to stay here longer with mine."

Tasha's eyes filled with tears as she went to hug Jerome. "How do you always know stuff like that?" she whispered as a tear fell down her cheek.

"I know you're still hurt by them, Tash. Just like I know you can't help but still love them too." Jerome held her tighter as he let her cry quietly on his shoulder. A knock got their attention as the two turned around and saw Senior standing in the doorway.

"Your mama wants some help with picking out ornaments" was all he said as he continued to stare at them.

Jerome nodded before looking back at Tasha. "Go ahead, she said. I'll finish wiping down the counters and join you."

With Senior still in the kitchen, Jerome looked at him and then back to Tasha. "Okay" was all he said as he kissed her on the forehead and left to help his mother.

As Tasha turned around to grab a dishrag, Senior spoke. "It would take either a brave or foolish person to come here today. Which one do you think you are, Ms. Daye?"

She smiled as she wiped down each of the countertops. "Both."

Whether Senior didn't like or was confused by her answer, Tasha didn't know. She only knew that she didn't care as he asked her directly, "Why both, young lady?"

"I've had to face worse than you, Senior, so I guess that would make me seem brave to some. But a part of me foolishly hoped that you would finally try to see me today, not my job or whatever rumors you've heard—at least for your son's sake. I was a fool to hope for that much." Folding the dishrag and placing it next to the scrubber by the sink, Tasha looked at Mr. Grant sadly as she walked away to join Jerome and Evelyn.

IT HAD BEEN YEARS SINCE Tasha even had a Christmas tree up, so she had more fun than she thought she would helping Jerome and his mother decorate their tree. After learning that some ornaments were handmade by Evelyn when Jerome was little, Tasha took extra care in picking them up and putting them gingerly on the tree. There was one ornament she couldn't take her eyes off. It was not much bigger than her palm and a swirl of neon purple, pink, and green. On one side of it there were three fingerprints that were in the shape of a snowman, but what caught Tasha's attention was the letter 'E' written in cursive around the smiley snowman. "Did you make this Rome?" Tasha asked with a grin.

Holding up the snowman so that he could see it, Jerome shook his head and reached out to take the ornament from Tasha.

"This one is Eva's. She made it when I was little."

Out of the corner of Tasha's eye, she could see Evelyn looking over at them and felt bad for bringing up a sore memory. "It's okay. We don't have to hang that one up. I'll find another one," Tasha offered as she searched in the large brown box.

"Jerome, hang it up," Evelyn instructed as she walked over to the two of them. Tasha looked up at the older woman as Jerome did as he was told, and she saw Evelyn doing her best not to cry. "That's one of the few things Eva left behind."

The room was silent for a minute as everyone stared at the now fully decorated tree. As another Christmas song played on the radio, Mr. Grant went to flip on a nearby switch and they all watched as the glow from the white lights made all the ornaments shine brightly.

"Thank you for today, Rome," Tasha whispered as Jerome smiled at her and took her hand into his.

The confrontation that she kept expecting to happen never did, even when Jerome kissed Tasha on her check in front of his parents as she brought him a cup of hot chocolate from the kitchen later that evening. Mr. Grant didn't bother saying another word to her, or anyone else that evening, except to say goodbye after Evelyn loaded them both up on leftovers as they were leaving.

"I will share this with my roommates tomorrow, Mrs. Grant," Tasha promised.

"Okay baby girl. Jerome, you drive safe out there, ya hear?"

"Yes ma'am. I love you," he replied before giving his mother another hug.

DRIVING IN SILENCE as Jerome took her home, Tasha almost fell asleep from all the good food settling in her stomach and the sound of the car humming as it went along the quiet roads. But once they reached her place, even as tired as Tasha was, she didn't want Jerome to go.

He helped her bring everything inside, and Tasha took her time putting all the food in the fridge just so she could sneak glances at him. Finally, she asked him softly, "Do you have plans for later tonight? Maybe we can watch a movie before you go?"

Tasha wanted to cringe at how desperate she sounded, but if it meant that Jerome would stay longer, she didn't care.

He looked at her before grinning and kissing her forehead. "I can stay for one movie."

The two snuggled up together on the couch with a thick throw blanket covering them as Jerome searched the On Demand stations for a good movie to watch. Tasha fought to stay awake, but being so close to Jerome, smelling his familiar scent, proved to be too much for her. Tasha looked up at his smiling face one last time before she finally went to sleep wrapped in Jerome's arms.

Chapter Eight
Can We Talk?

J erome

Weeks had passed since Tasha had agreed to be his girlfriend, but he really didn't notice much of a change. He wanted to take her out on a 'real' date, but between her schedule at The Fast Fix and photoshoots, they had a hard time matching each other's schedule to go anywhere. Deep in thought at the ASL center, Jerome tried to focus on his class, but he couldn't after reading Tasha's last text:

Hey Rome!
Do we really have to go to the movies tonight?
I'm already pretty tired from the 2 senior shoots I had today.
-Tash

He wanted to believe that was the reason Tasha was trying to get out of their first official date, but Jerome could not shake the feeling that there was more to her wanting to cancel on him. The small thought of Tasha not wanting to be seen with him, the golden PK, was inching its way into his head, and Jerome didn't like how that made him feel. Purposefully ignoring her text seemed like a smart move, but now the idea that Tasha might regret agreeing to date him made Jerome feel sick, and he had to respond.

Quickly getting up as the teacher was instructing another group of students on the board, Jerome slipped out of the classroom and turned down the hallway to call her. After a few rings, he got her generic voicemail and sighed as he left a message:

Hey Tash, I was looking forward to seeing you tonight. We talked about going to see this movie days ago, but if you can't meet up, then I guess I'll just see you next week.

Bye.

-Rome

He felt like an idiot saying that, but Jerome knew Tasha would call him back if he told her he wouldn't see her this week. Ever since Thanksgiving, she had no problem with snuggling up to him at his place after working at The Fast Fix. Sometimes he would even drive to her spot and Rachel or Alexa would let him into the apartment before they went to bed, so he could wait on the couch for Tasha to get home and shower.

"Jerome? Is everything okay?"

Turning around, he saw Betty looking up at him and Jerome sent her a small smile. "Yeah, just . . . leaving a message for my girlfriend." He still grinned like a fool when he said 'girlfriend' out loud, but Jerome didn't care. He just wished that he could spend more time with Tasha as his girlfriend.

"She must be pretty special, guessing from the look on your face right now."

"I like to think that she is."

"Okay, we'll see you back in class tonight then?" Betty asked. Jerome nodded as he put his phone away before going back inside.

An hour after the class ended, he still hadn't heard from Tasha, and Jerome was trying not to get annoyed. He called again, and this time the line went straight to voicemail. That little voice he'd spent all day ignoring was as loud as ever now, telling him that girls like Tasha would only see him as a good friend, that they'd never seriously date him, and that he was stupid for believing her when she said she wanted to be his girlfriend.

He didn't bother with saying goodbye to anyone, as all his insecurities made it hard for him to function. Once Jerome was in his car, he realized he didn't want to go home. There was no one waiting for him there, and being there now would only remind him of the person he had yet to hear from all day. So Jerome drove around until he found himself at the movie theater.

Jerome quickly parked his car and got in line to buy a ticket. The concession stand line wasn't long, so he went and ordered a small popcorn and a fountain drink. Just before the previews started, he turned his phone off and began watching the movie. Jerome felt uneasy almost as soon as the movie ended. And he knew it wasn't because he'd had too much popcorn earlier. Once he was in his car and on his way home, he remembered to turn on his phone, and almost immediately Jerome saw the screen light up. He had received another message from Tasha.

I took a nap in between shifts.
Can't wait to see you later :-)
-Tash

That explained why she didn't answer his voicemail, and Jerome was now wondering what would happen when he told her what he did. He was almost tempted to make a trip to SweeThangs, just to avoid telling Tasha the truth. But it was already early evening, and he wouldn't make it there and back before she finished working at the truck. Not sure what to do, Jerome thought about calling someone for advice and realized that other than his mother and Eva, there was no one he could talk to. Until an idea formed in his head and Jerome followed it all the way to Bottom's Up.

He inched into the parking lot and waited until he saw a line of people at The Fast Fix. Then he quickly got out of his car and went inside. Jerome paid the entrance fee and went to the bar. His prayers were answered when he saw the bartender, Kym, from his first visit. She saw him waving at her and walked over. "Soda guy? I thought you'd be a one-timer in here."

Jerome rubbed the back of his head as he looked at her sheepishly. "Me too, but I was hoping you could help me with something?"

She squinted at him before asking, "Is it illegal?"

Jerome's eyes widened as he shook his head, "Nah sister, nothing like that," he explained, "I-I'm having a girlfriend issue and thought to get a woman's opinion."

Kym didn't hide her laughter from Jerome, but he was in too deep to leave now. He waited until she finished wiping her eyes and said, "Okay, I'll hear you out, but you gotta buy something. Can't let my manager see you sitting up here not drinking."

Jerome took out a twenty. "Can I start a soda tab?"

Kym threw her head back and laughed.

JEROME TOLD KYM AS much of the situation as he could from what happened earlier today. In between songs, he noticed two other girls were also next to him at the bar, listening to his story.

"So, now that I've heard from her, what should I say? What should I do?" he asked hopefully.

The first girl yelled," Be honest!"

The second girl side-eyed her friend, "Hell no! Just agree to whatever she wants to do, otherwise she's gonna think you were being hella petty."

Kym handed him another soda before she weighed in. "I would say do both. Text ya girl and let her know that you already saw the movie. Then ask her what she wants to do."

Jerome reached out for the soda bottle and took a few gulps. "I already know what she wants to do, that's why I was mad and went to see the movie in the first place." The girls turned their heads towards him, waiting for him to explain. "She doesn't want to be seen going nowhere with a PK kid," he said sadly.

"Did she say that to you?" the second girl asked Jerome.

Jerome shook his head.

"So why you think that's what's on her mind?"

"She keeps saying how she's tired from working late, but she always comes by late to see me afterwards. Why would she still come over to see me if she's so tired from work?" Jerome asked them.

Kym looked at him before shouting over the loud music, "Because she really likes you PK!" The other girls nodded, and Jerome looked at them, clearly confused. "Listen, we work five, sometimes six nights a week in this place, and the last thing we want to do is see anybody afterwards," Kym explained while mixing a drink for another customer.

"I don't even want to see my kids until I've at least had a shower after working in this joint!" the first girl said before fist bumping her friend. "Ya girl probably already feels bad for not spending enough time with you because of work. So she goes home, washes the day away, and drives to see you? Yeah, whoever this chick is, she really likes you. So don't go being like the rest of these clowns in here and letting your pride come between y'all."

Jerome saw the other girls nod again, and he looked down at his now empty drink. Reaching into his back pocket, he took out the last of his cash and gave each girl a ten-dollar bill. "Thank you, ladies, for the advice. I'll text her now."

The girls cheered as Jerome stood up to leave.

TO KEEP HIMSELF BUSY while he waited for Tasha to call him, Jerome played a few games on the gaming system that Tasha had given him. As he was about to level up, he heard his phone ringing. "Hey" was all he could get out.

"Hey, big head! I'm at the theater. You on your way?" she asked.

Jerome hoped what the girls told him earlier was true. He walked out of his apartment to his car before answering Tasha. "Yeah. See you soon."

SEEING THE FILM FOR the second time that day, Jerome tried his best to be as into the story as Tasha was, but he couldn't do it. Once the movie ended, the two left the theater and Jerome could feel the weight of guilt on his chest. Tasha stole a few glances at him as they exited the theater, but other than that, she said nothing. The quietness between them now felt different, not how they usually were at his place.

"Is everything okay?" Tasha finally asked him. She stopped walking and looked up at him before Jerome answered.

"I want to say yes, but that would be a lie." Tasha continued staring at him, but Jerome said nothing else.

"Since we got to the theater, something has been off. I know that I've been busier than usual, but Rome . . . Did I do something to upset you?"

Seeing the small bags under Tasha's eyes, along with the slight crease forming on her forehead as she looked up at him, waiting for his reply, made Jerome feel disgusted with himself.

How could I doubt for a second that she didn't really want to be with me? "Tash? No, you did nothing. This is all me, okay?" he explained.

"What do you mean?"

Taking her hand into his, Jerome led them to a nearby bench, and the two sat down. "Earlier today, we kept missing each other's calls. I got frustrated, because I really wanted to see you this week." Tasha listened patiently as Jerome let out a deep sigh. "After not hearing from you for hours this afternoon, I came to the theater and saw the movie by myself."

Looking at Tasha and waiting for her to yell at him or smack his arm—anything to show her disapproval of his behavior—Jerome instead felt her wrap both of her hands into his as she closed her eyes. "Really Rome? I said I would see the movie with you. What made you decide to see it solo?" she asked.

Jerome let the warmth of her touch wash over him as he finally admitted his innermost thoughts. "Well, I thought you didn't really want to go out with me. You know, in public. Being that I'm the son of a preacher and all." He realized how crazy it all sounded now that the truth was out there, but Jerome wasn't done. "I thought you were just saying that you were busy when I would ask you to go out to places with me, you know, instead of saying that you really didn't want to be seen out with me."

Feeling Tasha pull her hands away from him, Jerome hung his head and waited for the break-up speech to start. When almost a minute went by and she had said nothing, Jerome brought his head up to look at Tasha.

Her eyes were on him, lips firmly in place, and he soon realized that she was waiting for him to look at her before speaking. "Rome, I wouldn't lie to you. To be honest, I'm not good at lying. When I say that I'm busy, I mean that." Tasha's glance softened as she continued talking to him. "I get that you have some insecurities about things, and that's why you felt the need to do what you did today. But Rome, if you make me waste money again coming to see a movie that you've already seen, we gonna have a problem!" Tasha's laughter drew the attention of a few strangers as they walked by, but Jerome could only stare at her.

"So, you're not mad?" He finally asked.

"A little, yeah. Mainly because I rescheduled catching up with my girls tonight so that I could watch this movie with you. I haven't seen much of them either." Confusion must have shown on Jerome's face as Tasha explained, "It's not just you I haven't seen, you know. With my new clients, having to drive to different locations, spending more time late at night editing, as well as learning all the not so fun parts about being a full-time freelance photographer, I'm missing out big time on having a social life."

With a schedule like that, it's no wonder you were napping in the middle of the day. And here I was, letting my pride lead me around by my spiteful nose. "Tasha, I'm sorry. Really, I didn't know."

She looked up at him before resting her head on top of his shoulder. "Me too. I should have done better at managing my schedule so that we could see one another more."

Jerome thought back earlier to what the girls at BU told him, and he had to ask, "If your schedule is so hectic, why do you still stop by the apartment to see me? You end up falling asleep an hour after getting there anyway."

He almost didn't hear her reply, as Tasha buried her face into his chest. "I don't know . . . I guess seeing you at the end of the day makes all the craziness worth it somehow."

Jerome wrapped his arms around Tasha and placed a kiss on the crown of her head.

TASHA

The small town that Tasha grew up in didn't offer much, but this Christmas Eve, it had everything that she could ever want.

Looking out the window from her bedroom as she finished her third glass of wine that day, Tasha couldn't stop grinning. The view of several palm trees twinkling from the many white tea lights that adorned them made the small pond gleam. But the star of the show for Tasha was the newly installed twelve-foot angel that almost blindingly shone around the townhomes surrounding it. Even as the sun was setting, the rays bounced playfully from the colored glass panes that made up the heavenly figurine.

Not sure if it was her newfound holiday spirit, or that lingering "L" word feeling she got from being in Jerome's arms, Tasha was coming around on this whole celebration of Jesus's born day. Which, if she felt like being honest, wasn't all that much of a shock. At this point in their official relationship, Tasha was considering it the price of admission from agreeing to date a preacher's kid. How that even happened remained a mystery to her. She never saw this kind of love in her life, and to have found it in the aspiring Christian rapper while working as a tutor at his daddy's church was enough to make even a hardened cynic like her call a truce with the OG. *At least until Easter,* Tasha thought to herself with a smirk.

Tasha knew her girls were going to tease Jerome the minute he arrived for their Christmas Eve dinner tonight, and Tasha hoped he would be okay with that. For the last week, she had been going straight to Jerome's after working at The Fast Fix, even on Saturday nights. Alexa and Rachel had been commenting on her late-night visits at his place, so much so that Tasha finally stopped trying to convince the two that she and Jerome weren't "sinning until dawn" and just took the joking from her best friends in stride.

At least this dinner will be way more casual than the one I went to for Thanksgiving at his folks' house. Thinking back to that event weeks ago, Tasha placed her now empty wine glass onto the high end dresser in her room before taking her phone out of her pocket and dialing up a new friend. "Hello Mrs. Grant!" .

"Well, hello there baby! How you been?"

Tasha walked from her room to join her friends in the living room. "I'm doing okay. How do you like the framed portraits?" she asked. After Evelyn expressed such an interest in the portraits she took of Jerome when the two of them visited Bejon Beach, Tasha did a little more editing and made sure to mail out her top favorites after having them framed for Evelyn as an early Christmas gift.

"I love them! Thank you," Evelyn told her. "But you could've just brought them over to the house yourself. You didn't have to spend all the money on shipping them here." That was the same thing Jerome said when she told him what she had done, but Tasha did not want to test her luck with seeing Pastor Grant uninvited. Things were good between her and Jerome, and the last thing she needed was to get into it with his daddy just before Jesus's alleged birthday.

"I wanted you to have the whole white glove photography experience." At least that part was true.

Evelyn's praising her photos on Thanksgiving warmed Tasha's heart, and she wanted to show her appreciation for that feeling the best way that she knew how.

Hearing a knock at the door, Tasha said goodbye to Evelyn as Rachel opened the front door, and she soon heard Alexa let out a low whistle. "Who says PK's don't know how to show up to a party!"

The second Tasha turned around to see what the commotion was all about, she immediately burst out laughing. Jerome walked in wearing a Santa hat and a small red bag over his shoulder. The festive green sweater that he donned had more than one set of jingle bells on it. When he sat the bag down onto the countertop, Jerome jumped up and down, causing the bells to ring out throughout the house. Seeing him all merry and bright made the extra work she did to secure his surprise Christmas gift worth it.

"And a ho, ho, ho to you too, Saint Nick," Alexa joked as Tasha wasted no time going to Jerome and wrapping herself in his arms. Jerome kissed her forehead, and as Tasha looked up at him, she heard a clicking sound. Looking over to her roomies, Tasha rolled her eyes as Rachel held her phone out and made a thumbs up sign with her free hand.

"I hope y'all are hungry, because we've been hard at work today cooking all this food," Alexa announced proudly after their impromptu selfie.

Tasha looked up at Jerome and grinned. "I'm starving."

JEROME

Spending Christmas Eve with Tasha and her friends was turning out much better than he'd imagined. Jerome got to talk more openly with them about his sister, and Tasha was more eager to receive kisses from him too. Each time Jerome took out the mistletoe that he'd brought in his Santa bag, Tasha would giggle before leaning in to give him a kiss on the lips. "How long will you two be at your parents' house this week?" Jerome asked Alexa, as the four of them now sat comfortably on the living room couch after dinner.

Alexa looked at Rachel and groaned, "Until this one here pops off at the mouth to my mama again. Then we out!" Everyone laughed as Rachel jumped up from the couch.

"You know ya mama don't like me! She always throwing them back-handed compliments out like my hearing don't work! And I ain't forgot about her asking you about your ex last year either . . ."

Jerome watched as Alexa reached out and pulled Rachel back down to the couch before giving her a few quick kisses on her cheeks. "I know and I'm sorry, babe. This year, if she starts something, please come find me so we can leave, okay?" Instead of answering, Rachel leaned in to give Alexa a kiss.

Jerome then unwrapped himself from Tasha's arms and went to his Santa bag. Taking out the small gifts that he'd bought for Alexa and Rachel first, he looked down at the other box inside before glancing over at Tasha on the couch. *She doesn't even know that I got her something. I'll wait and see what happens later before giving it to her.*

Quickly rubbing his free hand over the thighs of his jeans, Jerome walked over to the girls and stood in front of Alexa and Rachel. "Thanks for inviting me over today."

Handing each of them a red envelope, he watched as they both tore into them and leaped off the couch once they saw the gifts inside.

"Rome! You didn't!" Rachel squealed. Looking over at Tasha, Rachel quickly asked, "Is it okay if I call him that? I don't want to overstep, sis."

Everyone watched as Tasha sang, "It's more than fine. He's fine, you're fine, I'm fine."

Alexa hollered at the sight of her friend as Jerome attempted not to grin.

"What did Saint Rome get y'all, anyway?" Tasha managed to squeak out before hiccuping, finally getting Jerome to join Alexa in laughter.

Rachel leaned over the couch and shoved a Ms. SweeThangs Cupcake Bakery gift card in Tasha's face. "We will ring in the New Year with some sweet cupcakes!"

Alexa stared down at the four tickets Jerome bought her for *Love is Love* , a local off-Broadway musical. "Tash told me you had a friend that performs there, so I looked up their name and found the next show that they had a role in. Hope you like it," Jerome added shyly.

Alexa looked over at him and beamed. "I love it," she said as Rachel pulled her up from the couch. "Bring it in Rome!" she shouted, as Jerome switched seats with Tasha so Rachel and Alexa could both wrap their arms around him, engulfing Jerome in a hug. He peeked over at Tasha and saw her clapping and cheering at the sight. The two ladies separated from Jerome and snuggled even closer to Tasha on the couch.

"What did you do?" Rachel asked Tasha.

Confused, Tasha looked her friend up and down before asking, "What are you talking about?"

"What did you do to land the golden PK?"

Jerome slowly scooted down to the far end of the couch, very much curious to see where this talk was going to go. Tasha now looked between both of her friends, before pouting, "What do y'all mean? I was just my regular old self, and he came into my life. With plates of home-cooked food!" She then pointed at Jerome, whose eyes widened as the three women turned their attention to him.

"Ah! So it was you that did the seducing," Rachel cackled gleefully.

Jerome gulped, and Alexa leaned forward toward him as she spoke. "Yeah, it was him alright. Tash is too stubborn to make the first move." He watched as Alexa looked at both of them before turning her attention back to Tasha. "So he lured you in with his good looks and his mama's home cooking. Was that what happened, Tash?"

He watched as Tasha nodded quickly while Rachel and Alexa laughed. Tasha then stood up, winking at Jerome before turning down the hallway. Too focused on watching her walk away, he almost didn't hear Rachel speak. "We've never seen Tash so happy, especially this time of year."

"And we have you to thank for that, PK." Alexa told him. Despite his best efforts, Jerome's chest puffed out more than he meant for it to.

"Look at him, all full of himself!" Alexa said to Rachel.

"He should be! You know how hard it is for Tash to let people in," Rachel reminded Alexa. Jerome could feel the atmosphere change, more so when Alexa looked down the hallway, just past the wall-length Christmas tree and back to him. Rachel spoke again, and this time Jerome couldn't mistake the edge in her voice, even as she whispered, "Tash has been our A-1 since day one. And Lord knows she has been through more hurt and heartache than anyone should ever go through."

Jerome sat up quickly as Alexa narrowed her eyes at him. "So if you ain't serious about our girl, you better be honest now and end it. Because we will end you if you hurt her, PK."

He tried to speak, but Rachel cut him off. "You seem like good peeps, despite your daddy and them other fools at Christ's Corner, so we've been quiet. But Tash has never been in a serious relationship before. And we need to know, what are your intentions with her?"

Jerome didn't have time to speak, much less defend himself, as they all could hear Tasha coming back down the hall. She had changed into a holiday onesie, red and green, with gold stars all over it. "Thank you, Rachel, for this onesie! It's so comfy!" Jerome grinned like an idiot as he watched her twirl around, showing off the onesie.

"I'm glad you like it, sis."

Jerome felt the girls staring at him and all but bolted from the couch. Walking over to Tasha, he took her hand into his and sat her down at the barstool where his Santa bag still sat. Jerome's nerves were a bit shaken up after his 'chat' with Rachel and Alexa, but he decided to go through with what he had planned and reached into the bag, handing Tasha a tiny gold box. "We didn't talk about getting each other anything, but I wanted you to have this." He looked on as Tasha took the lid off the small box and shot her eyes back up to his.

"It's no big deal. Besides, you're always at my place, anyway. It just made sense," he explained as she looked back down at the key inside. Jerome watched and waited for Tasha to say something as she placed the lid back on the box and sat it on the counter.

"Thank you," she whispered. Tasha then hopped out of the barstool and wrapped her arms around Jerome's neck, causing him to sway in order to regain his balance. He laughed as she kissed both of his cheeks and his forehead.

"You're welcome."

TASHA

Her head throbbed more than expected the next morning, but Tasha managed to wake up on time to check on her Christmas gift to Jerome. It was still on schedule, and knowing that put a little pep in her step as she went to her bedroom to finish up a few more photo edits before Jerome stopped by to pick her up. Hearing her phone ring,

Tasha saved the work on her computer and answered cheerily, "Happy Holidays! Tash on the line."

Jerome's chuckle into the receiver made her blush. "Are you almost ready?"

Looking away from her computer to the clock on her nightstand, Tasha smiled as she answered his question. "I'm about to get dressed now. Door's open."

"I'll be there in a few."

They ended the call, and Tasha went to her closet to find something to wear. Remembering how chilly it was earlier when she took out the trash that morning, Tasha pulled out a few sweaters to choose from, along with leggings and jeans.

After staring for a few seconds, she grabbed her favorite pair of dark wash denim jeans and a thick gold sweater. Turning on the holiday station on her phone, Tasha started getting dressed while listening to the playlist.

After getting dressed, Tasha went back to culling and editing from her last photoshoot. Feeling someone staring at her, she looked up from her laptop and found Jerome standing in the doorway to her bedroom. From the look on his face, he'd been there for a while. Tasha had left the door open for him, so she wasn't surprised that he was already in the townhouse. She was surprised that he'd stopped just at her doorway instead of knocking on her bedroom door.

Smiling up at him, she saved her work again and turned off her laptop. Tasha then grabbed her phone and bag before walking toward him.

She was about to tip her head back to give him a peck on the check, but once Tasha was within arm's length, Jerome reached out to her and wrapped an arm around her plush waist, bringing her closer. As she gasped, almost dropping her bag, Jerome bent down to kiss her fully on the lips. Before this, they had been keeping it mostly PG, nothing over the top. Tasha didn't know if that was mainly for him or for her, but when his tongue swept across hers, she had decided then and there that it had been for her sake. Tasha's hands soon were around Jerome's neck as she deepened their kiss. If he hadn't released her, they would still be in each other's arms, making out like teenagers.

"Merry Christmas," Jerome finally said, before breaking out into a smirk.

Tasha took a little longer to reply. "Y-yeah. Merry Christmas to you too," she breathed out. Jerome led Tasha out of the apartment with his hand at the small of her back.

She fidgeted getting her house keys down from the key rack before locking the front door and making their way to his car.

GOING TO THE GRANTS' this time, Tasha wasn't nervous at all, and it must have shown.

"You're not still, you know, drunk?"

She squinted her eyes at him and bit back a laugh. "Wow, you really don't drink at all, do you?" she said to Jerome before taking his hand into one of her own as Jerome led them inside his parents' house.

"Ms. Daye, good of you to stop by again," Pastor Grant said as they entered the living room, never taking his eyes off the TV screen.

"Thanks for having me!" Swinging their entwined hands together, Tasha brought Jerome's hand to her lips and kissed it softly. "I'm going to see if I can help in the kitchen."

"You can first stop making googly eyes at my son and give me a hug."

Hearing Evelyn's voice behind her, Tasha grinned as she let go of Jerome's hand and walked over to the older woman. Admiring the new updo that Evelyn wore with her red wrap around dress and black kitten heels, Tasha said cheerfully, "Merry Christmas Mrs. Grant!"

Evelyn's single diamond earrings caught the light in the living room as she raised her head up to Tasha and smiled pleasantly. Feeling the warmth that radiated from Evelyn as she tightly embraced her, Tasha closed her eyes. As the women hugged, Tasha could see another car pull into the driveway, and she smiled. *They are right on time. Thank you, Lord!*

"You sure are in good spirits today, baby girl!" Evelyn said to her.

"I just feel like this season I have so much to celebrate," Tasha explained quickly as she heard a knock on the door. Jerome was already heading to answer it, but Tasha walked quickly back toward him, reaching out and grabbing his hand.

"Mrs. Grant, I think you should get that," she suggested. Both men then looked over at Tasha as there was another knock on the door.

"Well, let me go ahead and answer it then," the older woman chuckled.

She and Jerome stepped aside so Evelyn could open the door. He stared at Tasha before finally asking, "What is going on Tash?"

She didn't get a chance to answer him as Evelyn's cries were heard throughout the house. On the other side of the door were three people that Evelyn hadn't seen in years: her daughter Eva, Eva's daughter Evelyn Mae, and Eva's husband, Marcus. Each of them stepped into the house and the corners of Tasha's eyes stung from the sight. Looking up at Jerome, Tasha watched him stare at the guests as they all took turns hugging Evelyn before he looked down at her.

"Did you do this?" he asked.

Nodding, Tasha explained. "A few days after Thanksgiving, you were in the shower when your phone rang. I thought it might have been your mama, so I answered it. And that's when I met the other woman in your life," Tasha teased before continuing. "After that, it was too easy. Just an exchange of phone numbers, lots of texting, planning, and top secret secrecy. Oh, and a few frequent flyer miles from Alexa and Rachel."

Jerome stared at her before leaning down to leave a firm kiss on her temple.

"Merry Christmas," Tasha told him sweetly, before Jerome went to give Eva a hug.

She watched as he talked with his sister and her family. Feeling someone stare at her for the second time that day, Tasha looked around the room before her eyes landed on Pastor Grant. Meeting his glare, Tasha grinned and almost laughed out loud as he huffed before turning back around in his chair to look at the TV.

Finally, Eva and her daughter made their way toward her. Shaking off the pettiness that Pastor Grant had just given her, Tasha knelt down and signed 'Merry Christmas' to Evelyn Mae before introducing herself in ASL like she had been practicing. The younger girl giggled at her before telling Tasha, "I'm a CODA! My Daddy hears some too." Then she leaned in closer to stage whisper, "but he pretends not to when we're on the subway." Tasha looked up at Eva and Marcus and smiled again.

"Thank you for helping us come down here, Tasha," Marcus said slowly.

Evelyn Mae spoke again, "He practiced saying that for days!"

Tasha tried not to smile, but when she saw Eva was smiling, she did so too. Looking from Eva to Marcus, Tasha made an admission with her hands. "Me too."

Seeing the thumbs up from Marcus made her laugh even harder as Evelyn grabbed her and Eva's hands and led them into the kitchen.

* * *

SHOCKING EVERYONE AT the house, Pastor Grant did not say one out-of-pocket remark. He even allowed Jerome to lead in grace.

Tasha looked on in awe as Jerome translated everything he said with his hands. Since there were more people at the dining room table than normal, Tasha had to squeeze in beside Evelyn and Eva. Jerome sat next to Pastor Grant and across from his niece, who loved talking to her uncle with her hands.

"She really is going to make me practice harder from now on," Jerome said after Evelyn Mae asked him another round of questions.

Everyone laughed at that before Tasha tried to talk to both Marcus and Eva.

"Jerome taught me some words . . ." She paused before remembering what she practiced earlier that week. "I want to learn more."

Marcus and Eva looked at one another and smiled. Evelyn Mae had no trouble saying the first thing on her mind, as she looked at Tasha and then back to Jerome, signing as she spoke, "When you marry Uncle Jerome, he can teach you everything, Ms. Tasha."

Pastor Grant was mid sip with his drink and almost choked as Jerome stared bug-eyed at his niece before he recovered and volleyed a question back at her. "You think I should marry Ms. Tasha?" he asked.

Tasha heard Evelyn gasp as the little girl nodded. "Besides, mama says that if Ms. Tasha hasn't left you yet, then she either loves you or she's crazier than a bessie bug."

It was Tasha's turn to hide her laughter, as Jerome looked at his sister with a slack jaw while Marcus scolded Evelyn Mae with his hands too fast for Tasha to try to follow. Tasha looked around at everyone at the table before closing her eyes and shaking her head.

* * *

TASHA AND JEROME WORKED together silently cleaning the kitchen after dinner, while Eva and Marcus sat in the living room, sharing pictures of Evelyn Mae with Jerome's parents. After they finished cleaning the kitchen, Tasha packed all the leftovers, making sure to give Eva and her family the lion's share, before joining the others in the living room. Evelyn Mae fell asleep an hour later, bringing the reunion to an end for the night. They were the first to say goodbye, as Eva held a sleeping Evelyn Mae in her arms.

"We will be here for the whole week, so you can see Evelyn Mae every day, okay Mama Evelyn?" Marcus said, as he gave his mother-in-law a big hug.

"I still can't believe this Tash," Jerome said, as they went to the car and put the leftovers inside while Marcus and Eva said their goodbyes.

"So, you're not mad that I answered your phone without asking first?" she asked him as they closed the car door and made their way back to the house.

Jerome shook his head as he stopped at the front door. "Answer my phone all you want. I've got nothing to keep from you."

She was dead set on laying another smooch on him, but the Holy Ghost must've known where it would lead them because as she was leaning in, Jerome opened the front door. Trying not to frown, Tasha looked on as Jerome handed the car keys back to his brother-in-law. They all watched as Marcus unlocked and opened the back passenger side door for his wife and sleeping child. He then got into the driver's side of the car and put on his seat belt before starting the engine and driving away.

Seeing Evelyn trying not to cry, Tasha thought it would be best to give her a moment alone. "Can we sit outside for a little while?" she asked Jerome. He looked at Tasha and smiled softly before opening the front door again.

* * *

EVELYN

I just knew that Tasha was a blessing! Having both of her babies back in the house for the holidays filled Evelyn with a joy she hadn't felt in years. Watching her husband fall in line was a little nice too, but she didn't want to focus on that too much. Instead, she watched her babies be with the loves in their lives. Evelyn thought about what her namesake had said over dinner, and a smile slowly spread across her face. She hadn't wanted to get her hopes up about Jerome and Tasha jumping the broom just yet, and here comes this eight-year-old, saying it out loud for all the grown folks at the table. And though Tasha may have laughed at the time, she did not seem all that against the idea . . . *Out of the mouth of babes. Lord, if it is your will, it will be done!*

Looking around at her house, Evelyn saw that the dishes and food were all cleaned and put away thanks to Junior and Tasha. And with her husband back in his chair, watching the football game, Evelyn was happy, though she realized that Jerome and Tasha were missing. Knowing her son, Evelyn knew exactly where she would find them. Walking into the kitchen, Evelyn quietly slid open the window above the dishwasher. Sure enough, she could see the two lovebirds sitting out on the front porch. *I knew it!* Not bothering at all to hide, she peered out the window to see what they were up to. And her son, forever making Evelyn proud, was sitting on the small bench as Tasha lay her head on his shoulder.

"I gotta say Rome, this Christmas was pretty exceptional," Tasha said softly.

Jerome kissed her forehead, and that got a small squeal from Evelyn as she continued to watch the two. "Yeah, it was a great Christmas this year. I hadn't seen mama smile like that in forever."

Hearing her son's remark brought tears back to Evelyn's eyes. Tasha stared at Jerome before she spoke again. "Even when little Miss Evelyn Mae announced I should marry you, or admit to being crazier than a bessie bug?"

Jerome rolled his eyes as Tasha quietly laughed. Silence fell over them again, and Evelyn was just about to close the window when she heard Jerome ask Tasha, "What was your favorite memory from this Christmas?"

Evelyn and Jerome waited as Tasha seemed to think over her answer. "You really want to know, uh?"

"Yeah, I want to know. What was your favorite memory from Christmas this year?"

"Each moment that I had with you." Evelyn quickly brought a hand out to cover her mouth after hearing Tasha's answer. Jerome went to kiss Tasha on the cheek, leaving Evelyn grinning from ear to ear as she finally slid the windowsill down.

Thank you, Lord! My baby may be getting married after all.

JEROME

For the first time in a long time, Jerome did not want to leave his folks' house. Spending time with Eva, Evelyn Mae, and Marcus on Christmas truly was a blessing. He stared down at Tasha as he held her close on the tiny bench at the front of the house and enjoyed the silence between them. It had only been two months since they began dating, and he was seriously seeing a life with this woman. Jerome spent days lately writing bars for his first album—at work, at home, and even in between his workouts. But nothing he penned seemed to fully express how he felt about being her man.

Yeah, Tasha was hard sometimes - he saw that first hand with her sisters a while back. At first he didn't get why Tasha was so quick to use violence instead of her words, and if Jerome was being honest, it worried him. But the more he got to know her and see the world that she had to learn to live in, Jerome understood.

He didn't like it, but he at least knew why Tasha would react that way with certain people. And once Jerome came to realize that, all he wanted to do was to provide her with endless days of peace, the same as she did for him when they were together.

Tasha had no idea just how much solace she brought into his world. How her honesty and sometimes strange but always on point perspective guided him, especially these days when trying to talk to Senior. She had a way of speaking to him about things he already thought he knew, as someone who grew up in the church. And the way she almost instantly bonded with the two other main women in his life was something he was thankful for too.

At the dinner table earlier when Evelyn Mae spoke about him marrying Tasha, Jerome felt as if his thoughts were being laid out at the altar for everyone to see. He tried not to look at Tasha too much afterwards, scared that she would see right through him.

"Rome?" Tasha's voice lazily called out to him, and Jerome kissed the crown of her head.

"Yeah?"

"You know I'm not the most religious person and all, but I gotta say, being with you right now really feels like a gift." She then untangled herself from Jerome's arms and sat up to look him in the eye. "I don't have a lot of good Christmas Day memories, but I want you to know that I really enjoyed today. Thank you."

Jerome's heart swelled as he listened to Tasha share her feelings with him. "Why are you thanking me, Tash? When you're the one that helped Eva and her family come visit for the week—I feel like I should be thanking you." The seriousness he saw in her eyes had him rooted to the spot.

"I never knew . . . never let myself think that I could have moments like this. With someone like you, and I-I . . ." Tasha briefly shut her eyes and lowered her head before lifting it and looking at him again. "I want you to know how much it means to me, to have you in my life these last few months."

With his heart now in his throat, Jerome held her gaze. "Tasha, I lo—" Her lips were on his before he could say what had been on his mind for weeks. And as much as he wanted to say those words to her, Jerome couldn't help but get caught up in the feeling of her lips against his. The taste of peppermint reached his tongue as Tasha opened her mouth to explore his, and Jerome instinctively brought a hand up to caress her cheek. Up until this morning, the two would only give each other small kisses on the cheek, or Tasha would surprise him with a quick peck on the lips. Though when Jerome heard a small moan leave her lips, he wanted to spend the entire night seeing what other sounds he could get Tasha to make.

The fact that they had only been a couple for a few weeks was irrelevant. He knew a blessing when he saw one, and when Jerome tore his lips away from Tasha's and found her staring his way, he was sure of it. Seeing her eyes soften while trying to catch her breath almost took all the self-control he had left. He leaned in closer to Tasha and pressed his lips to her forehead. "You have no idea how much you mean to me."

Jerome wanted to feel more of her warmth. Her hands made their way to the back of his head, but it wasn't enough. A slight breeze whirled fast between them and as Tasha scooted closer, causing Jerome to send another prayer of gratitude to the heavens. Wrapping his arms around her to bring her even closer, Jerome kept his eyes on Tasha as she softly kissed his cheek. "Maybe we should go back inside?" she suggested.

The scent of peppermint still lingered in the air after she spoke and Jerome shook his head. His nose brushed alongside hers before he gave Tasha another kiss. "I want to stay here."

Not giving her a chance to protest, Jerome pressed their lips together once more, greedily pushing his tongue inside Tasha's mouth. Another moan, louder than the one before, vibrated from her mouth to his and Jerome groaned. The porch swing creaked beneath them when he reached his free arm out, grabbing Tasha's knees to bring her legs across his lap. With each rise and fall of her chest against his, Jerome grew warmer and warmer.

"Rome..." she whispered.

Jerome paused, willing himself to look at Tasha again. He found her staring at him with her mouth slightly parted. Wanting to make sure that he wasn't doing too much too soon, Jerome started to ask her if this was okay, until he noticed Tasha bringing her lush lips together. His eyes zeroed in on Tasha even more when she bit down on the corner of her bottom lip. She closed the distance between them again, and before long, Tasha's hands were frantically pulling him closer, lightly scratching at the nape of his neck. When the tips of her fingers touched the top of his burning ears, Jerome had made up his mind to scoop Tasha up and carry her back to his ride to take them back to his place. Because there was only one place he wanted desperately to be inside, and it was not his folks' house.

"Jerome! Tasha! Don't y'all catch a cold out there talking about nothing!"

The two jumped apart slightly from the sound of Evelyn's voice calling out to them from the kitchen, and Jerome had to clear his throat for the second time that night. "Yes, ma'am!" He looked over at Tasha, and the two of them chuckled.

"I guess we better get back inside then," Tasha said sheepishly.

Jerome watched as Tasha swung her feet out before standing up to turn to face her. He extended a hand toward her. He knew she didn't need his help to get up, but he wanted to feel more of her warmth before going back in the house. As she looked up at him and smiled, Tasha accepted his hand and Jerome knew that this was how he wanted things to be between them, forever. Walking to the front door, Jerome opened it and waited for Tasha to step inside first as he looked up at the evening sky.

Thank you, Lord, for all the blessings you have bestowed upon me this Christmas.

NORMALLY, FOR NEW YEAR'S Eve, Jerome would help his father with preparing his sermon for the New Year's service. This year the two of them were speaking even less than before, and Jerome decided whatever happened between them now, it was in the Lord's hands. He had been dutiful and patient, even offering an olive branch, only to have it snapped in his face. He wanted to be with Tasha and saw no reason why he shouldn't.

So, when Jerome realized Senior would not be asking him to help with the New Year's service, he accepted Tasha's invitation to a New Year's Eve party at a local club with her friends.

After hearing from Rachel that New Year's Eve was Tasha's favorite time of year, Jerome planned. For the first part of his plan, he had to see his mother, which is why he offered to take her out for breakfast after Sunday service the day after Christmas. Rushing through his morning workout and quickly showering before putting on clothes, Jerome was at his parent's house a full hour earlier than expected.

As he let himself in with his spare key, Jerome waited on the couch for Evelyn to come out of her room. Once she turned the corner, walking while putting on a pair of earrings, she jumped back, clutching her chest.

"Jerome! Why are you so early?" she asked, more than a little startled.

He got up from the couch to walk toward her before kissing both of her cheeks. "What? I can't be early for a breakfast date with my favorite lady?" Jerome watched as she eyed him.

"Boy! I gave birth to you, and I know when you're up to something. What is it?"

Speaking slowly to make sure that he got the words out right, he answered, "I want you to be the first to know that I am going to ask Tasha to marry me." He watched as Mama's eyes widened and she hopped slightly before wrapping him tightly in a hug.

"Are you sure? You really want to?" she asked as Jerome continued to nod. "Oh baby! I am so happy for you!"

"Why are you making all this noise this early in the day, Evelyn?" he heard Senior ask.

"Oh, hush up and go back to sleep!" Evelyn said, as she heard her husband getting out of the bed. She speed walked back to Jerome, taking a hold of his hand. "Let's head on out for that breakfast you promised me."

As she pushed them toward the door to leave, the weight of what he was about to do in the next few hours hit him, and he looked to his mother before asking her, "Am I supposed to be nervous before I do this?"

She looked at him and reached out to touch his cheek, "Nervousness is good. That means you know how serious this is, baby."

"How serious what is?" Senior now stood behind the two of them, squinting his eyes at Jerome.

Done with tiptoeing around his daddy, Jerome locked eyes with Senior. "I am going to ask Tasha to marry me. Tonight." Jerome watched as Evelyn lowered her eyes from Senior's glare. "I knew I wouldn't get your blessing, so I decided to celebrate with Mama today over breakfast instead of asking you for it."

"You right! I will not give you my blessing to go through with this!" Senior shouted.

"Why won't you give them your blessing, uh? Jerome loves that girl, and even the blind can see that she feels the same about him," Evelyn pleaded with Senior. "Have you even prayed on this issue at all Jerome?" she added. They both watched as he shook his head.

"Troubling the Lord about what I already can see with my eyes and feel in my soul is a waste of time."

Walking toward Jerome, Senior pointed his finger at him as he continued, "That Ms. Daye is not a woman who walks with Christ, and if you marry her, you will not have my blessing!"

Jerome looked Senior directly in the eye. "So be it, sir."

After having breakfast with his mother and driving her back home, Jerome prepared for the second part of his plan. Once he was back at his place, Jerome finally had enough courage to look at the ring that he'd gotten from his mother over breakfast. It was the engagement ring that Senior had given to her, just before they got married. He stared at the ring as it sat, encased in the small red box, on the dresser in his bedroom. *But what if it doesn't fit on her finger?*

Deciding that the meaning behind the proposal outweighed the wearability of the ring itself, Jerome grinned as he closed the box before getting dressed to go out. *I'm really going to ask her to be my wife.*

Chapter Nine

New Year's Eve Changes Everything

achel

R   "Baby! Come on already!" she shouted to Alexa, who insisted on changing sneakers for a fourth time before they left the house.

"She's like this every year. Let's just go wait in the car," Tasha suggested.

Rachel looked over at her friend and smirked. Since making things official with Jerome, Tasha had been way more laid back than she could ever remember seeing her. Even her outfit choices had changed, for the better in Rachel's opinion. Usually, Tasha would throw on a solid jumper with a pair of kicks and some big hoops. This evening, however, her friend donned a sequin black and gold dress that stopped just a little below her knees, to go with a pair of big tear-shaped gold hoops. Instead of sneakers, Tasha wore a pair of black wedge shoes that Rachel wanted to be mad about, but even she had to admit that they made her friend's New Year's Eve look complete.

"Y'all better wait for me! I'm the one with the tickets, anyway," Alexa called out before strutting into the living room.

Biting her bottom lip as she took in the sight of her love in a pair of fitted jeans, a button down satin blouse with only three buttons done, and the new kicks that Rachel gifted her for Christmas, she felt her annoyance all but melt away.

"See, you know I'm always worth the wait baby! Why you even tripping about the time, anyway?" Alexa closed the distance between her and Rachel as she placed her hand on the small of Rachel's back.

Tasha giggled, "Yeah, I guess you cute. Can we go now?

Rachel looked over at Tasha and laughed. "Yeah, let's roll out!"

"Let's get this New Year's Eve party started!" Alexa said, smirking as she held onto Rachel before walking out of their house.

TASHA

Where is Jerome?

Lightly tapping her left heel and looking around, Tasha tensed up for a second as Jerome made his presence known by wrapping her into a hug from behind. "Told you I was here," he said, as he kissed her cheek.

After hearing his voice, Tasha briefly closed her eyes as she relaxed into his embrace. Instead of letting each other go, the two shuffled forward to get in line for the New Year's Eve party being held at Cloud 9, the only club in town large enough to put on such an event.

Jerome kissed her cheek again, and Tasha felt her face get hot. She wasn't sure if it was from the pre-gaming drinks she'd shared with Rachel earlier or from simply having a man that loved doting on her in public every chance he got, but Tasha wasn't going to complain.

"Hey PK!" a woman yelled from behind them in line. Jerome broke his hold on Tasha before turning around to see Kym waving at them. He waved back and grinned.

Tasha stared and somehow kept her stank face away before asking, "How do you know Kym? Did y'all go to school together?"

Seeing him try not to blush, Tasha reached for his hand. "Let me guess, you had a crush on her back in the day, uh? You can tell me," she teased him gently. Just as he was about to answer her, Kym stepped out of the line and stood beside them.

"So, this is your girl? Hey Tash."

Quirking an eye between them, Tasha greeted Kym and spoke again, "I didn't know y'all knew each other."

Jerome chuckled as Kym explained, "Well, this one here shared a few bars with me in the club one time, then a few weeks later he came in asking for advice about, well, you."

Looking over at Jerome and trying not to be surprised, Tasha asked, "When was this?"

"Do you remember when we had that talk after going to the movies? It was that night," Jerome confirmed.

Kym laughed as she looked over at the couple. "Yeah, he came in and ordered a few sodas to talk about how you didn't want to be seen with him in public."

Tasha's eyes gazed up at Jerome's and he squeezed her hand.

"Looks like we was right, uh PK?"

Jerome nodded, "Thanks again for the advice, Kym."

The woman looked at the couple again and smiled. "Anytime! It's nice to see love win."

"Stop by The Fast Fix anytime, sis. I'll be sure to hook you up with anything you want," Tasha offered. Kym grinned as she turned away to rejoin her friends in line.

"So . . . you really went to Bottom's Up looking for relationship advice?" Tasha teasingly asked Jerome. He kissed her quickly on the lips.

"Well, yeah. I'm still new at this and didn't know who else I could ask," he admitted, making Tasha giggle.

The line moved again, and the bouncer checked their IDs before letting them go through the metal detectors. Once they were cleared to enter the club, Tasha took his hand again and smiled. "I'm glad you went to the girls. And I'm so glad to be here, celebrating the beginning of a New Year with you, Rome."

Jerome leaned in to kiss Tasha, and it felt like time had frozen. He soon wrapped her in his arms, and Tasha let herself get lost in the feel of his soft lips. She was ready to find a corner and spend what time they had in this year left locking lips with Jerome.

"Dang Tash! Let the man breathe and come join us!" Alexa shouted at them over the music.

Jerome broke their kiss and Tasha pouted. "Ignore her Rome . . ." Tasha purred sweetly into his ear, as she trailed her fingertips up from his chest to caress his cheek. Just as she could see him about to give in, she felt someone interlock their hands into her free hand.

"Y'all still have ninety minutes before the ball drops to do all that!" Rachel pulled Tasha away and laughed as Jerome reached out for her.

Soon, the two were dancing along with everyone else as the DJ played one club banging track after the other. Her feet hurt, but Tasha was not going to sit down and leave Jerome out on the floor. Luckily for her, Jerome pulled her close and leaned down toward her ear, "Let's grab a seat before the countdown starts."

She nodded and let him lead the way to a nearby empty table, but once there, they noticed that there was only one chair left to sit in. It did not surprise Tasha at all when Jerome pulled the chair out for her, but she knew he was tired too. A sly thought came to her, and when Jerome brought the chair closer, Tasha turned the seat around and walked toward him, forcing him to sit.

"Tash, your feet gotta be sore. Stop playing and sit down."

"Relax Rome, I'm going to sit," she assured him. Before he could get up to offer her the seat again, Tasha turned around and sat directly on his lap. "Thank you for the seat," she said, before kissing him on the cheek. For a few seconds, Tasha thought maybe she had gone too far, until she felt his hands wrap around her waist. Leaning back, happier than a bee in a new flower full of pollen, Tasha ignored the few folks staring at them and enjoyed the feeling of being in Jerome's arms.

The bar staff was walking around with trays of champagne in glasses to pass out to everyone before the countdown began, but Tasha had already planned to ring in this New Year without a drink. It made sense, as Jerome didn't drink and she didn't want him to feel uncomfortable. So she was more than a little shocked when he released his hold on her to wave down one of the servers and took two of the flute-like glasses. "Rome, we don't have to toast to the New Year. Just being here with you is enough for me."

"It's okay, I already called a car service for us later," he replied. With sixty seconds left before the ball dropped, Jerome handed her a glass and asked, "What do you want for the New Year?"

Blinking back tears, Tasha answered, "More times like this with you!" She then asked him the same question, and he grinned.

"Would I be lame for saying the same thing?" Tasha laughed as Jerome brought her in even closer.

"11 . . . 10 . . . 9 . . ."

"You are anything but lame!" Tasha told him, before kissing his cheek.

"7 . . . 6 . . . 5 . . ."

Jerome looked down at Tasha, his eyes almost twinkling as the two joined everyone else in the final countdown. ". . . 3 . . . 2. . . . 1 . . . HAPPY NEW YEAR!"

Feeling his lips land on hers, Tasha thought her heart couldn't get any fuller.

PATRICK

Looking at his social media as Rookie danced in front of him, Patrick was ready for the club to close. BU was all but empty as most people went to Cloud 9 to ring in the New Year. The girl he'd asked to go with him to Cloud 9 turned him down because she said that she had to get up early for the New Year's service at church the next day. *Seriously? She knows she's a ho! Trying to get on God's good side for the New Year.*

The song ended, and as Rookie started to walk away, he grabbed her by the wrist. "Did I tell you we're done? Again."

After the last song, the house lights came on, and Patrick walked outside to wait for Rookie to get dressed. Once he saw her being escorted by the night bouncer, he waited for the guy to walk back inside before driving up to her. She opened the door, and as she closed it, Patrick pressed his foot hard on the gas. Watching her lurch forward, he laughed. "Before we have some real fun, we're going to finish celebrating the New Year."

Her eyes widened before asking, "Where? Everything is already closed."

Looking her over sharply, Patrick laughed again. "You thought I was gonna be seen somewhere with you? Hell no, girl!" Rookie turned away from him, but he could still see her in the window, wiping her eyes.

After driving a few miles out, Patrick stopped and pulled into the local park. Cutting off the ignition, he let himself out. As he waited for Rookie to join him, Patrick saw a black sedan pull up not too far away and park in Jerome's apartment complex. A short man could be seen exiting the driver's side of the car and quickly opening the door behind him. Jerome stepped out and handed the man what looked like a credit card before walking to the other side of the car.

"Hurry up girl! I ain't got all night!" he yelled at Rookie as he kept his eyes on the vehicle.

Rookie finally got out of the car, but not before he heard giggling in the distance. They watched as Jerome and Tasha, holding hands, slowly made their way toward the park. The two looked up and froze when they saw Patrick. He sneered at them and turned to spit in front of Rookie's feet. The girl stepped backwards and almost tripped as she looked up at him.

"Well, what do we have here? I guess even a PK can be a heathen when he wants to, uh?" Patrick drawled out as he openly eyed Tasha in her short black dress.

Tasha was about to walk toward him, the same fire in her eyes as the night she threatened to tase him outside the club. This excited Patrick, but the moment was short-lived as Jerome took hold of her wrist and pulled Tasha away.

"Nah, PK, let her come on over here. I got something she might like," Patrick taunted. Seeing Jerome's frown deepen made Patrick laugh. "What? You thought you were the only one into thick pudding? Hey, if it's good enough for you, then it's gotta be good enough for the rest of us!"

Rookie sat on the bench behind Patrick and hung her head.

"Why are you even out here with this jackass, Rookie? You can do better," Tasha finally said. Rookie didn't answer as she looked down directly at the ground.

"Unlike you, fatty, Rookie here knows her place."

Jerome stepped in front of Tasha and Patrick stepped back a few feet from the sight of the storm brewing in the other man's eyes. "I'm only going to say this once, Patrick. Whatever issue you have with Tasha, it's with me now. Watch how you speak to her," Jerome told him gravely.

"Let's just go, Rome," Tasha said to Jerome gently, as she tugged on his elbow.

Patrick looked on as the two turned around and headed back to Jerome's apartment complex. "Happy New Year to y'all too!" he called out as the two kept walking away.

Taking out his phone, Patrick found a track he wanted to hear before sitting down next to Rookie. "It wasn't working for me at BU, so I'mma need you to twerk here."

Rookie looked at him, unshed tears in her eyes. "You can't be serious! Ain't it bad enough I ain't make no money tonight 'cause of you?!" she wailed. He turned up the volume on his phone and waited as Rookie wiped her face again before removing her jacket.

JEROME

Everything was going perfectly that New Year's morning, and then Patrick had to be at the park. Jerome learned early on that violence was not the answer, but last night, he was ready to test that theory. After they walked back to his place, Tasha hardly said a word. She took a shower and grabbed her linens soon after. By the time Jerome got out of the bathroom and went to say goodnight to Tasha, she was already asleep on the couch.

Part of him, no matter how small, couldn't help but wonder if what happened was a sign from God to not ask for Tasha to be his wife. Senior's words echoed in his head all night, and Jerome got little sleep thinking about them.

When morning finally came, he was surprised to find a more cheerful Tasha waiting for him in the living room. She had her twists in two fluffy buns, with a few loose strands on one side, showing off her signature side fade. Before he could turn around and brush his teeth, Tasha came over to him and wrapped him in a tight hug. "I'm sorry I went to bed mad last night," she murmured into his chest.

"It's okay."

"No, it's not. I let my worrying about Rookie and my anger toward Patrick ruin our first New Year's Eve together. I'm really sorry."

Tasha pulled away and looked Jerome in his eyes.

Even if I were mad, I wouldn't be any more, looking at her now.

"Hurry and get dressed. I want to take you out for breakfast," she told him cheerfully.

The shock must have shown on Jerome's face as Tasha added, "I kinda like being out in public with you. Showing you off to everyone and stuff."

Jerome laughed as he watched her trying to hide the redness that was creeping up on her cheeks. "Okay, let me get dressed."

THE LINE FOR A TABLE at Wayward's was long, but Jerome didn't mind waiting since Tasha used that time to entwine their hands together while looking down at her phone. A few minutes passed peacefully until he heard her gasp, getting his attention.

"What is it? Everything okay?" When Tasha said nothing, he peeked over at her phone and quickly covered his mouth with his free hand. Pictures from last night's party were up on Cloud 9's website, and someone had tagged them in a few of them. The pictures were mostly of them dancing, but the ones that he could see over Tasha's shoulder getting the most likes were of them just before midnight.

"Rome! What is your mama gonna think if she sees these?"

That I proposed, and you said yes. Which you didn't 'cause I didn't ...

Jerome carried the ring in his pocket this morning, in case a moment presented itself, but first they had to talk about these pictures. And he wanted to make sure that Tasha knew exactly how he felt. Acting quickly before they were called to a table, Jerome took Tasha's phone out of her hands.

"Wait! What are you doing?" she asked suddenly, trying to get her phone back from him.

Jerome kept typing and only gave the phone back once he hit 'send.' When she had her phone again, Tasha shrieked, gaining the attention of a few people around them.

"Jerome, that is NOT funny!" she hissed as she reread his post under one of their pictures.

Can I get a few of these printed out in wallet size please?
- Jerome 'JPK' Grant

"Good, because I didn't write it to be funny," he told her matter-of-factly.

They were finally shown to a table and given a menu before Tasha spoke again. "I should not have been drinking with Rachel before going out last night! This is bad, really bad, Rome." Tasha looked at her phone again and sighed.

"How is this bad, Tash? Everyone knows that we're together, and it's now their cross to bear if they don't like it."

He laughed again at the slack jaw on Tasha's face, which quickly changed into a thin line as she looked off behind Jerome's shoulder. Turning around, he noticed a few members from his church's adult bible study class as they marched over to where he and Tasha were sitting.

The first woman leaned against the table and spoke to Jerome while keeping her eyes on Tasha. "I guess the rumors are true after all. Wouldn't have believed them if I hadn't seen it with my own eyes."

Tasha jumped up from her side of the table and put her balled up fist to her side. "If you don't find your manners and put some distance between you and him right now, I'll be the last thing you see with those eyes."

Jerome tried to put his hands out between the women before addressing the two from his church. "Sisters, please leave us and enjoy your meals in peace."

"How can we do that? Knowing you were stolen from us good girls by that . . . that . . ." the second girl started to say as Tasha pushed Jerome out of the way.

"I dare you to finish that sentence. I fucking dare you!"

Remembering what happened between Tasha and her sisters at the church a few months ago, Jerome grabbed Tasha's hand and pushed his way through the women, exiting the restaurant.

Once outside, Tasha shouted, "This is what I was trying to avoid! This shit right here!" He watched as she paced the parking lot before looking at him again. "All those people will ever see when they look at me is my mama, my hood, and my last name."

Jerome walked up to her and placed her in a vice grip hug, trying to absorb all the hurt that she had inside. "Tash, I don't care what they see when they look at you. All I see is the girl that I want to be with. That's what matters, okay?" Feeling her nod against his chest, Jerome kissed the crown of Tasha's head before releasing her. "We can still order Wayward's pickup, right?" he questioned out of the blue, making Tasha smile.

THE TWO WENT BACK TO Tasha's to have their breakfast there. Tasha's giggles could be heard echoing down the hall as Jerome placed more kisses on her neck, slowing her down from unlocking the door. Soon they were inside, and Jerome went to the restroom to wash up again. As he came back into the living room, he saw Tasha looking down at her phone, face twisted and tears threatening to fall from her eyes any second.

"Baby, what is it?"

Tasha didn't even comment on him calling her 'baby' as she handed him her phone.

When he saw what people were posting under one picture from their night at Cloud 9, Jerome wanted to scream. Several photoshopped photos of them were under the original post. The most liked one being a picture of Tasha working at The Fast Fix and a cropped photo of Jerome with the caption 'Freak Nasty Special.' It wasn't just the crude photos, but the comments that made his hands shake.

I bet his mama is praying hard af for him rn, lol

How could PK have such shit taste?

I bet she lets him rawdog her anywhere.

They disgusting! Ijs, lol

Jerome couldn't read anymore as he placed Tasha's phone on the countertop. Reaching out to comfort her, Tasha flinched from his touch. Rubbing his hands to his temple, Jerome tried to keep his voice steady as he looked at Tasha. "I don't know what to say, Tash."

Hearing her laugh made his heart drop. "What else could be said?" She looked at him and wiped her face as the first tear fell. "Are you sure you still want to be with me? The disgusting, rawdog for attention girl?" she spat out.

Jerome looked at her incredulously. He reached out to grab her again, and seeing Tasha look away from him almost broke his heart. "Tash! I want to be with you. And I don't care what some pathetic, hate-filled folks got to say!" Reaching into his pocket, he dropped to one knee and watched as more tears fell down her face. "I've had this box, burning a hole in my pocket for two days now, and I'm done. Done with trying to find the right time to ask you." Tasha placed her hand over her mouth as she sobbed while looking down at him, shaking her head.

"Tasha Daye, please. Please be my wife." Jerome choked out.

Dropping to her knees and wrapping Jerome into her embrace, Tasha held his face into her hands and took a few slow breaths before speaking. "Jerome, I want to say yes, I do."

"Then say yes, please," he begged her as he placed kisses on her forehead and cheeks. As he kissed her one last time on the lips, Tasha wiped more tears away.

"I need more time, Rome, please understand. You have to know how I feel about you. But after today . . . I need some time, okay?" She explained to him gently.

Jerome opened his mouth to speak, but the two heard keys jingling at the front door. Helping Tasha get up to her feet and clearing his throat, they watched as Rachel entered, jumping in shock from seeing them already inside.

"As soon as I saw the pictures from last night, I called Alexa. She's at Cloud 9 now, Tash."

Jerome clenched his jaw as he slipped the box back into his pocket.

"Rachel, we have to stop her. I don't want her to lose her practicing license over this," Tasha said.

Jerome leaned down to give Tasha a kiss on the forehead and wordlessly walked out of her house.

TASHA

A week had passed since the picture incident, and Tasha hadn't left the apartment. Besides getting groceries and two pre-scheduled and paid-in-full photoshoots, Tasha spent every day indoors. Alexa and Rachel took turns checking in on her, and Alexa told her yesterday that she was selling The Fast Fix. Even as Tasha protested, Alexa stood firm in her decision.

"It was meant to bring in a little extra income, not to be used to tear apart your character, Tash."

Now having nothing to do and nowhere to go, Tash felt humiliated for a second time. Jerome called her every day but she couldn't bring herself to answer. That didn't stop her from missing him.

Instead, Tasha spent her time thinking over what to say to him and planning for his response. She wasn't upset over the pictures anymore. Well, not as much, but Tasha did want something from Jerome. Picking up her phone and pressing one, it was midway through the first ring when he picked up. "Can you stop by? I need to talk to you in person, please."

Jerome arrived an hour later, giving Tasha some much needed time to practice saying what she had planned. As she went to the door to let him in and saw him, it took all that was left in her to not run straight into his arms. Instead, Tasha stood back and let him enter. Closing and locking the door behind her, she began. "I'm sorry for how I left things last week. And I'm sorry for taking so long to return your calls."

Jerome stared at Tasha as she went on. "I wanted to ask you if you were free sometime this week? The weekend maybe?" When he tilted his head, Tasha felt the need to explain, "I know you asked me to be your wife. And before I give you an answer . . . I want to give you something else too." Praying that his silence meant that he understood what she was implying, Tasha waited for Jerome to speak.

"Does that mean you're saying yes?"

Tasha closed the space between them and crushed her lips against his. Backing him into the door, she didn't hold back as she pressed her body against his. Jerome tried to push her away, but Tasha wrapped her hands behind his neck and stuck her tongue down his throat, causing his hands to shake as he held her closer. Tasha then separated from Jerome and waited for his breathing to return to normal. "If you agree to come with me this weekend, I will be saying yes to more than just a ring."

Jerome locked eyes with Tasha and finally answered her. "Okay. Let's go away for the weekend."

Chapter Ten
Truthful Shores

T*asha*

She knew he was hers, but Tasha couldn't bring herself to go through with it. Watching Jerome as he held her hand while they walked along the beach, listening to the ocean's heartbeat and watching the sun set, she knew she would not have sex with him tonight.

A part of her wanted to, just to mark him so that the next woman he let into his heart would know that he'd loved her first. Tasha knew how messed up that thought was, and as the little voice got louder and louder in her head, urging her moral compass to shut up, be selfish and to take what was hers, she released his hand. It took Jerome a few steps to stop walking. The distance between them was necessary, otherwise what she was about to say may have never left her lips. "About tonight, I know what I said before, but I changed my mind."

Jerome looked at her before glancing out at the evening sky. She watched as he tilted his head just slightly down toward the shore and inhaled deeply. "Okay."

Tasha still didn't trust herself to touch him again, so she wordlessly walked next to him and the two went back to walking side by side along the shore. Every so often, she would feel his eyes on her, but Tasha said nothing else. Soon they reached the bed and breakfast that she'd booked for them that night and almost suggested that they stay somewhere else. *No, nope. You picked this venue and now you gotta deal with the fallout,* she told herself sternly.

Jerome led the way as they went back to their room, and Tasha's anxiety became their plus one as he used the keycard to unlock the door. The dimmed lights turned on as he placed the card into the electric slot, and Tasha wanted to grab her duffel bags and never look back at this place.

Everything was there, just as she ordered.

While they were away having dinner and walking along the beach, Tasha had paid extra for the owner of the bed and breakfast to leave them with a few items meant to make the night more memorable. She watched as Jerome took in the sight of chilling bubbly cider, strawberries and oranges dipped in dark chocolate, as well as two gift boxes. Before Jerome could reach out to pick up one of the boxes, Tasha sprinted past him and swooped them both into her arms.

"You, um, really went all out for tonight, uh?" Jerome asked Tasha, as he rubbed the back of his head and looked everywhere else in the room but at her.

"I just wanted it to be special." Tasha barely heard the words as they left her mouth.

Feeling all sorts of embarrassed, she went looking for her duffel bag to put away the now soul crushing presents she was going to give him. As she put the smaller box into her bag, Tasha felt Jerome's hands encircle hers, almost rooting her to the spot. The electricity was there in seconds, starting at the crown of her head and surging like hot liquid down to her toes.

"Every day I spend with you is special, Tash," he murmured into her ear.

She dropped the bag onto the floor and gripped the second box with both her hands. Her entire body now radiated with a need she didn't know was possible, and if Jerome didn't put some space between them soon, Tasha knew she would happily take back what she said out on the beach. Thinking fast, she remembered what was in the large box within her hands and asked, "Do you want to see a print from our last trip?"

Jerome let her go and Tasha gave herself a few seconds to let the blood in her body flow back to its original places before turning around and thrusting the box to his chest. She watched as he eyed her briefly before accepting and removing the ribbon from the light green packaging.

His mouth now agape, Tasha shared with him why she had this photo framed. "I'm still not sure what your style is as an artist, but this photo showcases all of you. As you are to me, anyway." She watched Jerome take in the way his eyes steadily gazed forward. With the evening rays creating a soft contrast between his skin and the simple scoop neck t-shirt he wore for the impromptu beach shoot, the gentle breeze that flowed around him made capturing the image feel effortless for her in that moment. Tasha felt her heart putting in overtime as it thumped faster than normal in her chest. "Everything that day was pretty great, but this shot speaks to me the most for our time together then," Tasha continued.

She remembered talking to him while taking those photos, the same way she did with all her clients during a normal shoot. When they started talking about the future release of his debut album, Tasha had asked him about his last track, 'Golden Days.' The look in his eyes, that quiet confidence that she saw was what made her take the photo, but once she got home and saw the photo again, Tasha picked up on everything at once. "I wanted to show you what I see when I look at you."

Jerome held the framed photo for a second more before putting it on the table next to the fruit and cider. He stepped toward Tasha, and she had to close her eyes to steady herself once more as he reached out to touch her chin with his warm fingertips. Using his fingers to level

Tasha's eyes toward him, Jerome asked gently, "What do you see when you look at me?"

The two held their gazes for a beat before Tasha whispered, "I see patience, hard work, thoughtfulness . . . and the love you have for me."

Jerome's jaw clenched as he blinked his eyes quickly. "So why did you change your mind about tonight?"

A tear slid down her cheek before Tasha could wipe it away. "Because tonight, I finally saw you as a husband. Just not mine." With the truth now out, there was no going back. Tasha knew that, as she saw the crestfallen look on Jerome's face. He was only agreeing to her terms because he loved her, and Tasha loved him too much to deny him the wedding, marriage, and family that she knew he wanted. *Finish it Tash, don't leave him wondering*, she willed herself.

"Why Tash? Why?" Jerome croaked out as his hand slipped from her chin.

Tasha stepped back two feet, and she saw Jerome flinch. That hurt her more than she wanted to admit at the moment, so she focused on what she needed to say instead. Wiping more tears from her eyes, Tasha told him honestly, "You want to marry me, and I want to be with you. Marriage was not something I ever saw happening for me, but I never thought that I would fall in love either. So I convinced myself that you would be happy with whatever I could give you right now. That's how I came up with this plan to ask you to come away with me tonight. Then we would just elope and leave town. It sounded great in my head, and I was ready to suggest it to you. Until I looked at you on the beach." Jerome inhaled deeply and exhaled slowly as he looked at Tasha and waited for her to finish. "I realized that if you and I were to do that, if we were to sleep together now, you'd regret it. Because a part of you knows I don't want to get married. Then what would happen when you find a wife? What will you say? When she asks about your body count?"

Catching her completely off guard, Jerome laughed out loud. "I didn't think those lyrics would come back to haunt me someday," he said bitterly.

Tasha remembered the body count line from the 'It Counts' track on his album and shook her head. "I didn't mean to —"

Jerome closed the space between them and brought his lips to hers, catching Tasha off guard. She didn't know where he learned to kiss, but Tasha knew that if she didn't find the strength to end this now, they would spend the rest of the night making the moon blush. Gently, Tasha placed her hands against Jerome's chest, pushing him away just enough to clear her head. "Jerome, we can't," she whispered. "I know you love me, and right now, you're probably scared to be without me. I know this because that is how I felt when I knew you wanted to marry me."

"But Tash—" he tried to interrupt, but Tasha kept going.

"Right now, I have no doubts that you would screw me right out of my draws to get a ring on my finger in the morning. But what would happen then, Rome?" Seeing him blink at her told Tasha his answer. "You haven't thought about the after, have you?" she asked him.

"T-the what?"

"The morning after. The day after. The year after."

Jerome slowly took a few steps away from Tasha as he sat at the foot of the bed in their room.

I should have given this to him first, she thought as she went across the room and picked up the bag again.

Grabbing the smaller blue box, Tasha closed her eyes and let out a small sigh as she turned back around and walked toward Jerome. She stopped a few feet in front of him before deciding to sit next to him. "When you asked me to marry you, and I asked you to give me time to give you an answer, I was scared. So scared of having to learn how to live without you again. Scared of losing you as a friend. Mainly, I feared hurting you by saying the first answer that came to mind when you asked me that day."

Letting that admission hang in the air, Tasha went on, "A few days after you proposed, I knew the next time we saw each other that you would want to hear my answer. While I was walking along the plaza after a shoot, I saw this in the window." Tasha's hands trembled as she gave Jerome the box, and for a second he didn't open it. Minutes seemed to pass before he finally removed the top of the box to reveal a smaller, velvet royal blue box. Taking that one out of the first box, Jerome gingerly opened it and snapped it shut almost immediately.

Tasha looked on as Jerome avoided her stare. The deep charcoal zirconium ring wasn't flashy by most folks' standards, even with the rose gold between the band. But the moment she saw it that day after her last photoshoot, Tasha wanted to give it to Jerome. Remembering the inscription she had added to the ring, Tasha sent a prayer up to the OG that Jerome didn't read it tonight before she explained, "I thought that if I gave you that ring, as a promise ring, that it would be enough for now." Jerome quietly wiped away tears from his face as she continued, "Because I love you, Jerome. So much that it hurts. But I don't think that I can give you the life you want."

Coughing to clear his throat, Jerome whispered, "Tash, I-I'm okay with eloping and starting our lives somewhere new or whatever . . ."

Tasha shook her head. "You say that now, but would you really be okay with it? Not having your mama or sister see us take our vows?" She watched as Jerome lowered his head. "Would you still be happy having to find new work when we moved to another town and have to put your dreams on hold, again? What happens when you tell me you want kids and I say 'not right now' for the third or fourth time? What about then Jerome?" She already knew the answer to all those questions, but seeing Jerome's narrowed brows after her last question, Tasha had all the confirmation that she needed. "You have no idea how much it's going to hurt me to see you move on, but you will," she finished as

Jerome opened the box and looked at the ring again before sitting it down next to him on the bed.

"So, you're giving me a ring and ending our relationship? Is that what's happening right now?" he confirmed flatly.

Tasha nodded as more tears fell down her face.

"You know I don't drink, but I really wish there was something harder than that sparkly stuff you got over there right now," Jerome joked, making Tasha lightly chuckle despite the tears.

Even as I'm calling things off between us, this man can still make me smile, Tasha thought sadly. "I want to be that wife for you. I want to give you that life—a beautiful wedding, an insanely happy marriage, and as many kids as I physically can. But I can't Jerome."

He then wrapped her into his arms and the two spent the night in one another's embrace before falling asleep.

Jerome awoke before Tasha the next morning and packed everything into his car, so all Tasha had to do was freshen up in the bathroom before they headed back home.

The four-hour drive was spent in silence as the two held hands and stole glances at each other. Before they knew it, Jerome was pulling up in front of Tasha's place and his grip on her hand tightened before the car came to a stop. They sat together for a few minutes before he undid his seat belt and got out of the driver's seat to make his way to her side of the car. Jerome opened the door for her, and as Tasha was getting out of the car, he had already grabbed her duffel bag and was walking by the main gate entrance.

Not wanting to leave his side just yet, Tasha let him carry her belongings up the stairs and to her front door. As she was looking in her messenger bag for her house keys, Jerome's voice almost didn't reach her ears as he softly requested, "Please, don't say goodbye to me Tash." Tasha paused as she pushed the key into the door lock and turned to face Jerome. He left little room between them, which is why when she brushed against him Tasha was not surprised to find her back already touching the door. "I heard you out last night, and I can even understand how you came to your choice. But right now I am holding it together by hoping that someday you'll be my wife. I just ask that for now, please don't say goodbye."

Feeling her eyes starting to sting again, Tasha slowly nodded. When she reached out to take her bags from Jerome, he handed them to her and quickly looked away. She silently put the bags down next to the entrance and watched as Jerome used the back of his hand to wipe at his face before turning to face her again, and Tasha instinctively brought a hand out to touch his cheek. Jerome caught her hand midair and stared at her so intensely that Tasha felt her heart leap into her throat. She knew the kiss was coming when he grabbed her waist and almost knocked her head back as his lips landed on hers. His hands seemed desperate to engrave every inch of her frame to memory, as Jerome gripped her waist and lower back.

She shook from the contact, trying to give him the time he needed to let her go. Just as Tasha's lungs were beginning to burn from the lack of air, Jerome released her and turned to quickly walk back to his car.

Completely wordless and on the verge of breaking down, Tasha picked up her bags and let herself in the townhouse.

What she was not prepared for was seeing her roommates lounging on the living room couch, drinking wine and eating nachos. Tasha said nothing as they both rushed toward her, neither one picking up on her bad vibes.

"Well, hello there Tash!" Alexa shouted. "Fancy running into you here." Her friend hiccupped and then chuckled at her own corny joke.

Pushing her way past Alexa, Tasha was already prepared to try to lie about the incident, but the Lord wasn't done with her yet. Rachel was skipping her way toward them as well, but she held a thick manilla envelope in her hands. "Sis! This came for you yesterday, but you were long gone! Probably making the preacher's kid sin somewhere."

Seeing the happiness and love in her friend's drunken eyes as they looked at one another in that moment and catching a glimpse of the return address on the envelope in Rachel's hands, Tasha dropped her bags and went to her knees. The wail that followed felt like it came from the deepest part of her soul and all the tears that she had been holding back that day finally came out.

Tasha's entire body shook as she sobbed out loud. Alexa and Rachel were on each side of her, trying to find out what they did wrong to make her cry.

"It's all me . . . I'm what's wrong." *Why couldn't I just say yes? Why can't I be happy?* Leaving her friends and her bags on the floor, Tasha slowly made it to her bedroom. When she did, she shut the door and locked it for the first time since moving in. Kicking off her shoes and crawling into bed, Tasha cried herself to sleep for the second night in a row.

Three Months Later...

"You've looked at that stupid thing every day since you got it in the mail," Alexa said to Tasha, who held her shiny blue passport as if it were a priceless jewel.

"It's not stupid! Took me a long time to finally get this baby, and I can't wait to fill it with stamps," she explained dreamily as the two made their way into the airport.

Tasha watched her friend glance around the ticket area before sighing, "Alexa, you know I'm coming back, right? It's just a six-month internship."

"You know your ass ain't coming right back! A six-month, PAID internship for one of the most up and coming global media companies? In Argentina, sis?!" Alexa looked at all her luggage and pouted. "You even saved up to buy that bougie-ass luggage."

Tasha looked down at her three suitcases and bit her lip. "Well, this luggage was a little pricey, but I had to! They suggested it in the orientation documents. Rebel Shots clearly stated to not skimp on protecting your photography gear, and I didn't want to fly halfway around the world half stepping . . ."

Alexa laughed, "You half stepping? Never!"

Tasha burst out laughing along with her good friend as Alexa did a cute two step. Tasha knew where the conversation was going next from the way Alexa looked at her phone before looking back at her. "I know you heard the latest on JPK by now. You surprised?" her friend asked gently.

Tasha had not only heard, but had gotten a phone call from Jerome personally before the news was officially announced. It was the last time the two of them had spoken to one another. After the cypher he took part in months ago went viral, an A&R rep reached out to him. They offered him a record deal with a major label in Atlanta that were looking to expand their business further into the south, and Jerome accepted it after meeting with a new company called W.O.K.E. He went to school with one of the co-owners back in the day, and they wanted to make sure the label that approached him was on the up and up, so his friend's company's legal team looked over the contract for him at no charge.

After Jerome shared the news with Tasha, he then congratulated her on the internship with Rebel Shots. Tasha asked about his mama and Jerome told her that Evelyn was doing alright, she was now in New York visiting Eva, Marcus and Evelyn Mae. The call was peaceful, and after not talking or seeing each other for several months, it surprised Tasha at how not awkward it was to talk to Jerome again. It almost felt like old times, before they were something more. Back to the days when they were just starting out as friends, and Tasha loved that feeling. Years may pass before she would ever get over what they almost had, but Tasha was hopeful that they could at least start over as friends someday.

She felt Alexa looking her way, and when Tasha turned toward her friend, she saw her sniffling. "Alexa, I promise I'll be back," Tasha tried to assure her as she went to give her now crying friend a hug.

"I-I know that Tash! Dang!" Alexa wailed. "It's just . . . girl! You've been through hell and you still keep fighting. Now look at you, on your first trip abroad, about to take the photography world by storm! How do you do it?" Alexa asked.

With her eyes now full with unshed tears, Tasha hugged her friend even tighter before letting her go. "I just do, Alexa. And my life ain't been all that bad." Tasha winked as she grabbed her luggage while looking down at her passport and ticket. "If I had given up and given in when I thought things were terrible, I wouldn't have this moment now. I guess you can say that I had faith that things would get better."

Alexa clapped, gaining the attention of a few people around them as she quickly threw her arms around Tasha again and kissed her cheek. "I know that's right! You better keep the faith, sis!" she shouted as Tasha walked to the ticket counter line.

Turning to look back at her friend one more time, Tasha waved to Alexa through her tears as Alexa waved back before finally exiting the airport. Wiping her face while standing in line, she closed her eyes and smiled.

I really am on my way. Finally.

Her feet practically floated to the ticket counter booth. Tasha handed the airline representative her documents. The woman took in her beaming face and asked while viewing her passport, "Is this your first trip abroad, Ms. Daye?"

Tasha's grin rivaled the sun as she answered, "Yes."

The representative then checked in Tasha's luggage and returned her passport, before letting her through to her designated concourse to wait for her flight.

Let's Discuss A Dove's Cry!

1. What feelings did this book evoke for you?
2. What other book(s) did this remind you of?
3. Share a favorite quote from the book. Why did this quote stand out?
4. What did you like best about this book?
5. What did you like least about this book?
6. Would you read another book by this author? (Why or why not?)
7. What do you think of the book's cover? (How well does it convey what the book is about?)
8. Which characters in the book did you like best?
9. Which characters did you like least?

10. If you got the chance to ask the author of this book one question, what would it be?

Don't miss out!

Visit the website below and you can sign up to receive emails whenever K. McCoy publishes a new book. There's no charge and no obligation.

https://books2read.com/r/B-A-VWLI-DGPTB

BOOKS 2 READ

Connecting independent readers to independent writers.

Did you love *A Dove's Cry*? Then you should read *Doves Cry Too*[1] by K. McCoy!

Can love keep a saint and a sinner together?

Shocking family news brings the now international yet reclusive photographer Tasha Daye back to her small hometown in Florida.

Everything is going well until she lays eyes on her first love, Jerome Grant.

And no matter how hard she tries to avoid him, the two are unable to stay away from one another. A new friendship between them blooms, but long kept secrets resurface, threatening to separate them for a second time.

Will Jerome and Tasha hold on to love, or will they break each other's hearts for the last time?

---

1. https://books2read.com/u/bO2Kxo

2. https://books2read.com/u/bO2Kxo

Read more at https://authorkmccoy.com.

Also by K. McCoy

MAGIX
MAGIX
MAGIX: Melodic Whirlwinds

Standalone
A Dove's Cry
A Season to Love
Cupid's Kiss
Holiday Bliss
Doves Cry Too
The New E.R.A.
Hits Keep Coming

Watch for more at https://authorkmccoy.com.

About the Author

K. McCoy wants to live in a world where people don't try to compensate artists with only exposure and every public restroom played either Lo-Fi or Classical music. Her stories (outside of the world of MAGIX) are those of awkward cute meets as well as sweet declarations and discoveries of love. Her poetry is known for their inspiring lines about mental health, self-love, body positivity, and quirky traits that are to be celebrated.

When she is not baking or playing DISCRETION with her friends, you can find her writing down new ideas and concepts somewhere sunny or discovering new music online. Her goals are to travel and to see as much of the world as possible and to continue writing amazing stories for her growing audience.

Continue reading, continue writing, and continue loving the process is not just a signature sign off for her blog posts, but a way of life.

You can find out how to connect with K.McCoy by visiting her on all social medias under authorkmccoy.

Read more at https://authorkmccoy.com/.